They weren't going to get married and have children.

Soon they weren't even going to see each other again. And the most important *weren't* on the list was the fact that they *weren't* in love.

Love, forever and ever love, was a recipe two people made carefully together: They met, were attracted to each other. Add sharing and caring, respect and honesty, and blend well. Sift in smiles and laughter and lovemaking. Simmer until hearts melt, then mesh into one entity strong enough to withstand the rigors of time.

Whoa, Alice thought. What was she thinking? She and Brent had two weeks together. Two short, safe weeks. There was no *forever* about it…right?

Dear Reader,

There's more than one way to enjoy the summer. By picking up this month's Silhouette Special Edition romances, you will find an emotional escape that is sure to touch your heart and leave you believing in happily-ever-after!

I am pleased to introduce a gripping tale of true love and family from celebrated author Stella Bagwell. In *White Dove's Promise*, which launches a six-book spin-off—plus a Christmas story collection—of the popular COLTONS series, a dashing Native American hero has trouble staying in one place, until he finds himself entangled in a soul-searing embrace with a beautiful single mother, who teaches him about roots…and lifelong passion.

No "keeper" shelf is complete without a gem from Joan Elliott Pickart. In *The Royal MacAllister*, a woman seeks her true identity and falls madly in love with a *true* royal! In *The Best Man's Plan*, bestselling and award-winning author Gina Wilkins delights us with a darling love story between a lovely shop owner and a wealthy businessman, who set up a fake romance to trick the tabloids…and wind up falling in love for real!

Lisa Jackson's *The McCaffertys: Slade* features a lady lawyer who comes home and faces a heartbreaker hero, who desperately wants a chance to prove his love to her. In *Mad Enough To Marry*, Christie Ridgway entertains us with an adorable tale of that *maddening* love that happens only when two kindred spirits must share the same space. Be sure to pick up Arlene James's *His Private Nurse*, where a single father falls for the feisty nurse hired to watch over him after a suspicious accident. You won't want to miss it!

Each month, Silhouette Special Edition delivers compelling stories of life, love and family. I wish you a relaxing summer and happy reading.

Sincerely,

Karen Taylor Richman
Senior Editor

Please address questions and book requests to:
Silhouette Reader Service
U.S.: 3010 Walden Ave., P.O. Box 1325, Buffalo, NY 14269
Canadian: P.O. Box 609, Fort Erie, Ont. L2A 5X3

Joan Elliott Pickart

THE ROYAL MacALLISTER

Silhouette®

SPECIAL EDITION™

Published by Silhouette Books

America's Publisher of Contemporary Romance

For my dear friend and agent,
Laurie Feigenbaum,
with special thanks for
understanding that authors
are mommies, too.

 SILHOUETTE BOOKS

ISBN 0-373-24477-0

THE ROYAL MacALLISTER

Copyright © 2002 by Joan Elliott Pickart

All rights reserved. Except for use in any review, the reproduction
or utilization of this work in whole or in part in any form by any
electronic, mechanical or other means, now known or hereafter
invented, including xerography, photocopying and recording, or in
any information storage or retrieval system, is forbidden without
the written permission of the editorial office, Silhouette Books,
300 East 42nd Street, New York, NY 10017 U.S.A.

All characters in this book have no existence outside the imagination of
the author and have no relation whatsoever to anyone bearing the same
name or names. They are not even distantly inspired by any individual
known or unknown to the author, and all incidents are pure invention.

This edition published by arrangement with Harlequin Books S.A.

® and TM are trademarks of Harlequin Books S.A., used under license.
Trademarks indicated with ® are registered in the United States Patent
and Trademark Office, the Canadian Trade Marks Office and in other
countries.

Visit Silhouette at www.eHarlequin.com

Printed in U.S.A.

Books by Joan Elliott Pickart

Silhouette Special Edition

*Friends, Lovers...and
  Babies! #1011
*The Father of Her Child #1025
†Texas Dawn #1100
†Texas Baby #1141
Wife Most Wanted #1160
The Rancher and the Amnesiac
  Bride #1204
△The Irresistible Mr.
  Sinclair #1256
△The Most Eligible M.D. #1262
Man...Mercenary...Monarch #1303
*To a MacAllister Born #1329
*Her Little Secret #1377
Single with Twins #1405
◊The Royal MacAllister #1477

Silhouette Desire

*Angels and Elves #961
Apache Dream Bride #999
†Texas Moon #1051
†Texas Glory #1088
Just My Joe #1202
△Taming Tall, Dark Brandon #1223
*Baby: MacAllister-Made #1326

Silhouette Books

*His Secret Son
◊Party of Three
◊Crowned Hearts
  "A Wish and a Prince"

Previously published under the pseudonym Robin Elliott

Silhouette Special Edition

Rancher's Heaven #909
Mother at Heart #968

Silhouette Intimate Moments

Gauntlet Run #206

*The Baby Bet
†Family Men
△The Bachelor Bet
◊The Baby Bet: MacAllister's Gifts

Silhouette Desire

Call It Love #213
To Have It All #237
Picture of Love #261
Pennies in the Fountain #275
Dawn's Gift #303
Brooke's Chance #323
Betting Man #344
Silver Sands #362
Lost and Found #384
Out of the Cold #440
Sophie's Attic #725
Not Just Another Perfect Wife #818
Haven's Call #859

JOAN ELLIOTT PICKART

is the author of over eighty-five novels. When she isn't writing, she enjoys reading, gardening and attending craft shows on the town square with her young daughter, Autumn. Joan has three all-grown-up daughters and three fantastic grandchildren. Joan and Autumn live in a charming small town in the high pine country of Arizona.

THE MacALLISTER FAMILY TREE

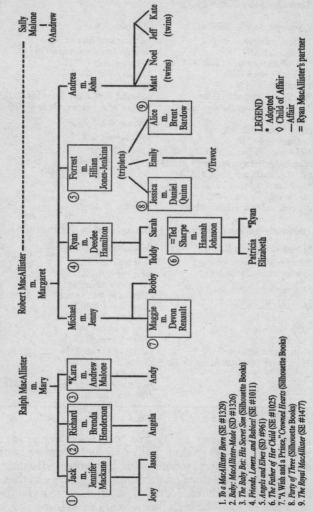

Sally Malone ――― ◊ Andrew

Robert MacAllister m. Margaret

Ralph MacAllister m. Mary

① Jack m. Jennifer Mackane
② Richard m. Brenda Henderson
③ *Kara m. Andrew Malone

Joey Jason Angela Andy

Michael m. Jenny
Bobby
⑦ Maggie m. Devon Renault

④ Ryan m. Deedee Hamilton
Teddy Sarah
⑥ =Ted Sharpe m. Hannah Johnson
Patricia *Ryan Elizabeth

⑤ Forrest m. Jillian Jones-Jenkins
(triplets)
⑧ Jessica m. Daniel Quinn
Emily ――― ◊Trevor
⑨ Alice m. Brent Bardow

Andrea m. John
Matt Noel (twins)
Jeff Kate (twins)

LEGEND
* Adopted
◊ Child of Affair
―― Affair
= Ryan MacAllister's partner

1. *To a MacAllister Born* (SE #1329)
2. *Baby: MacAllister-Made* (SD #1326)
3. *The Baby Bet: His Secret Son* (Silhouette Books)
4. *Friends, Lovers...and Babies!* (SE #1011)
5. *Angels and Elves* (SD #961)
6. *The Father of Her Child* (SE #1025)
7. *"A Wish and a Prince," Crowned Hearts* (Silhouette Books)
8. *Party of Three* (Silhouette Books)
9. *The Royal MacAllister* (SE #1477)

Chapter One

Alice "Trip" MacAllister stood outside the five-star restaurant engaged in a heated argument with her toughest opponent...herself.

She did *not*, she fumed as she began to pace, want to be here, taking part in the huge family dinner that would include the royal family of the Island of Wilshire.

Royal family. Her cousin Maggie was going to marry an honest-to-goodness prince, for crying out loud. Maggie had met Devon Renault on New Year's Eve while on duty in the emergency room at the hospital, and it had been practically love at first sight for the dewy-eyed pair.

It was now the first week in March, and Devon's family had finally managed to make all the necessary arrangements to enable them to travel to Ventura, California—the upscale city where the MacAllisters lived.

Unbelievable, Trip thought, continuing her trek. Ever since Maggie was a little girl she'd dreamed of marrying a prince, had made it her wish each time she blew out the candles on her birthday cake, and—ta-da—she was going to do exactly that...marry her Prince Charming.

She was happy for Maggie, she really was, but... The wedding would be held on the island in six weeks, and would be a gala affair with all the royal pomp and circumstance. And she, Trip MacAllister, in what must have been a mentally diminished state at the time, had agreed to attend.

But that was a nightmare to think about later. What had her nerves jangled to the point of near-hysteria now was that she was expected to attend the dinner inside this restaurant, was in fact late in showing up.

But she didn't want to be here. Family gatherings were not her thing, per se, hadn't been for as long as she could remember. She always felt uncomfortable, edgy, constantly ticking off the seconds until she could leave whenever she was surrounded by the multitude of MacAllisters.

And *this* dinner also included a royal family, for Pete's sake, who had just arrived early this morning. Devon's father, King Something...oh, what was his name? Chester. King Chester had decided it would be best to get acquainted with his son's fiancée and her family in a more relaxed setting rather than amid the hoopla surrounding the wedding.

Dandy, Trip thought with a sigh, as she stopped wearing a path in the sidewalk. But why hadn't she begged off? Even worse, she was wearing a dress she'd borrowed from her sister Jessica. A slip dress, Jessica had called it. It was skimpy and clingy and made her feel like a little girl playing dress-up.

She'd recently worn the one nice outfit she owned to Jessica and Daniel's wedding and couldn't show up in the same thing. The remainder of her wardrobe consisted of jeans, shorts and casual tops. Oh, yes, and the tacky polyester number that was the color of Pepto-Bismol that she wore when waiting tables at the café. Asking Jessica to loan her a dress had seemed like a good idea at the time, but this creation was absurd.

She was going home, Trip decided. She'd send

a message inside to her parents saying she had the flu, or a killer headache, or the chicken pox, or some lame thing, and hightail it out of there. Yes.

No, she thought in the next instant. That wasn't fair to Maggie, or to the rest of the family she was attempting to mend fences with after years of keeping emotional and physical distance between them. A goal that, in her opinion, wasn't going too well so far.

Get a grip, Trip told herself, patting her cheeks. *March in there, and smile while you're marching.*

Trip took one step toward the door of the restaurant, then halted in her tracks as a man came striding past, obviously not seeing her as he fumbled with a tie while muttering under his breath. He stopped two feet beyond where Trip stood.

"Dumb," he said. "Why does a man have to put on a tie to eat dinner? Who made up these rules? And who invented these god-awful things? It must have been a woman who hated men." He flipped one end of the tie around the other, pulled it through, then turned slightly as he shoved the knot to the top of his shirt. "There."

"It's lumpy," Trip said. "And the tail is too long and…you'd better start over."

"Well, hell," the man said, yanking the tie apart. "For two cents I'd ditch this shindig."

Trip laughed. "I'd ditch my party for one cent."

"Oh, yeah?" he said, looking at her for the first time. "Would you be dead as a post if you did?"

"In spades," Trip said, matching his smile.

Good grief, she thought, he was handsome. He was grumpy as all get-out, but he was drop-dead gorgeous, that was for sure. He was tall, probably six foot or more, had thick, black-as-midnight hair, rugged tanned features and the bluest eyes she'd ever seen, surrounded by long, dark lashes a woman would kill to have. Broad shoulders, long muscular legs, dark suit custom-fitted to perfection... Absolutely gorgeous.

"Well, I guess I've put this off as long as I can," Trip said with a sigh. "I'd better go in there, apologize for being late, and smile, smile, smile."

"Wait," the man said quickly and a tad too loudly.

"Wait?" Trip said, cocking her head slightly to one side. "Could you add something to that command so I know what you're talking about?"

"What? Oh. It wasn't a command, it was a plea. Would you help me with my tie? Then I'll go find my group, too, I guess. I'm already late, I'm probably in hot water and I don't dare show up without a tie."

"Well, I…" Trip started, then shrugged. "Sure. Why not?"

The man stepped closer, and Trip gripped the tails of the tie, her eyes widening for a moment as she saw that her hands were trembling slightly. She drew what she hoped was not an obviously steadying breath, then completed the task, giving the knot a pat when she finished. Before she could drop her hands, the man grasped them between both of his.

"Thank you," he said in a raspy voice. "I mean that. Thank you very much."

"You're welcome," Trip said, then met his gaze.

Dear heaven, she thought, she couldn't breathe. The heat from the man's work-roughened but gentle hands was traveling up her arms and across her breasts, causing them to feel heavy and achy.

Oh, mercy, now the heat was swirling throughout her, lower, hotter, pulsing deep. Those eyes. Those incredible blue eyes were like a mysterious ocean holding secrets yet to be discovered. They were pulling her in, making it impossible to move, or to think clearly. This man, this stranger, was…was dangerous, so blatantly, sensually masculine it was overwhelming.

"I…" Trip started to say, then realized she didn't have enough air in her lungs to speak.

"Look," the man said, his voice rather gritty,

"we're about to go our separate ways, now that we're going inside the restaurant, but I'd really like to know your name. Please? I'm Brent Bardow."

Brent Bardow? Trip thought. Why did that sound familiar? No, forget it. If she'd met this man before, she most definitely would remember.

"I'm Tr— I mean, I'm Alice," she said, after drawing in much-needed air. "Alice MacAllister."

"You're kidding," Brent said with a burst of laughter. "Did my name ring a bell?"

"Yes, but..."

"I'm Devon Renault's cousin from the Island of Wilshire." Brent's smile grew bigger. "Shame on you, Alice MacAllister. You don't want to go to the party set up for our families to meet before the big wedding bash."

Trip pulled free of Brent's hold, took a step backward and planted her hands on her hips.

"Shame on *me?*" she said. "I seem to recall that two cents would have been enough to get you to head south rather than go in there."

"Guilty as charged," Brent said. "Well, you and I are obviously the black sheep of the family. Black sheep who are very late in showing up for this shindig. Shall we go face the music? Everyone will be on their best behavior tonight so maybe we won't catch too much hell."

Trip laughed. "Don't count on it." She paused. "Okay, partner in crime, let's go."

The private dining room reserved for the party was enormous, yet managed to maintain a rather cozy atmosphere with its dark paneling. The crystal chandeliers were dimmed just enough to add soft light to the candles on the long, gleaming table, which boasted the restaurant's finest china and crystal.

When a still-smiling Trip and Brent entered the room, an immediate hush fell and close to forty pairs of eyes were riveted on the pair.

"Sorry I'm late," Trip and Brent said in unison, then looked at each other and burst into laughter.

"Your tardiness is not excused, Brent," Byron Bardow, Brent's father, said, scowling at his son.

"Well, they're here now," Jillian MacAllister said as she directed a rather speculative look at her daughter. "Dare we ask where you've been?"

"It was my fault," Brent said. "I was faced with a crisis situation." He ran one hand down his tie. "Alice was good enough to assist me in rectifying the dilemma." He grinned. "How's that?"

"Not worth a plugged nickel," Brent's mother, Charlane, said smiling. "But your excuses for being late, or not showing up at all, rarely are, dear." She swept her gaze over everyone seated at the table. "This is our son, Brent, who should be introduced to the members of this gathering, then given a test on the names to see if he'll be allowed to have dinner."

"Thanks a bunch, Mother." Brent chuckled. "I assume those two empty chairs are for Alice and me?"

"Indeed they are," King Chester said from the far end of the table. "Your salads are there. Sit down and eat and catch up with the rest of us."

Robert MacAllister, Trip's grandfather, had the place of honor at the head of the table, at the opposite end from the king.

"You look lovely this evening, Alice," Robert said. "That dress is very becoming."

Forrest MacAllister frowned. "I think she forgot to put *on* her dress. She's wearing a slip."

"Got it in one, Dad," Trip said, sitting in the closest of the vacant chairs. "It's all Jessica's fault. She loaned me this slip, then got in a huff about something and wouldn't give me the dress to wear over it." She shrugged. "What can I say?"

Brent settled on the chair next to Alice, mentally thanking whoever had arranged the seating for the evening.

"That's not true," Jessica said, laughing, then

looked at her husband, Daniel. "See what I went through growing up? This is a recording...it's all Jessica's fault. Trip was a master at getting me into trouble."

"Amen to that," Emily, the third member of the MacAllister triplets, said. "Remember the puppy Trip found and dragged home, not caring whether he wanted to come or not? Then told Mom and Dad that the mangy beast had followed *me*?"

"Let's not get started on those kind of stories." Robert laughed. "It's a pleasure to meet you, Brent. Let me introduce my family. As for a test on who is who, that's still open for discussion."

Brent nodded and smiled as Robert delivered the multitude of names.

Trip? he thought, only half listening to the names to go with the faces. Alice's grandfather had called her Alice, but her sisters had used the strange title of Trip, which must be some kind of rather weird nickname. To him she was Alice, because that's what she'd called herself outside the restaurant.

Alice, he mused. Like Alice in Wonderland, who embarked on a mystifying journey when she'd fallen down the rabbit hole and had no idea where she was going? Interesting thought.

He didn't want this beautiful woman to disappear, never to be seen by him again. She was exquisite. Tall, slender, about thirty years old, he'd guess, and she had big, brown eyes that were accentuated by her peaches-and-cream complexion. Her hair was blond, very short and just wavy enough to be extremely feminine.

That dress. Whew. It clung…what there was of it…in all the right places and seemed to change colors as she moved like…yes, like a lovely pastel opal.

He had a great deal to learn about the enchanting Ms. MacAllister and could not deny that he was looking forward to discovering the pieces to the puzzle.

Conversation around the table resumed, and the noise level was high as Trip and Brent concentrated on eating their salads.

"Trip?" Brent said quietly to Alice.

Trip flipped one hand in a dismissive manner. "Old news. Long story."

"I'm interested. Will you share your old, long story with me?"

Trip popped a radish cut to look like a flower into her mouth and shook her head.

"Ah, a secret, is it? This will be challenging." He stared into space for a long moment, then looked at Alice again. "Try this on for size. Trip is a nickname you were given at some point in your life before you became the lovely, graceful creature that you are. You were in a stage where you constantly fell...tripped...over your own feet. Did I nail it?''

"Not even close," Trip said, then followed the radish with a cherry tomato.

"Well, damn, I'll give this more thought. Unless, of course, you want to put me out of my misery and just tell me what the deal is.''

"Nope."

"How's the food at the Pop In Café, Trip?" her cousin Bobby asked.

Trip shrugged. "No one has died from it in the two months I've been waiting tables there. The only thing I've tried is the homemade pie and it's delicious.''

"Maybe I'll stop by and sample the pie," Bobby said. "If I eat in your area do I have to tip you?''

"Big time, cousin." Trip smiled.

"Forget it," Bobby said. "You still owe me two dollars and twenty-two cents for the lizard I sold you when we were kids.''

"I'm never paying for that crummy lizard." Trip laughed. "You failed to mention that it had been dead for a week before you convinced me to buy it. I thought it was sleeping in that shoe box you toted it around in, but the poor little thing had croaked.''

''That's why I gave you such a smokin' deal on it,'' Bobby said, grinning at her. ''My original asking price was five bucks when it was still breathing. Hey, I'm about to become a father. I need that two twenty-two to feed and clothe my firstborn child, Trip.''

Trip rolled her eyes heavenward. ''I moved back to Ventura over the Christmas holidays, and I already know that some things have not changed during all the years I was...where I was. I am not giving you the money, Bobby MacAllister, so put a cork in it.''

Laughter erupted around the table, and Brent smiled politely while gathering his data about Alice from what he had heard.

Curiouser and curiouser, he thought, was that Alice was a waitress at a place named the Pop In Café. A waitress? There was certainly nothing wrong with that profession, but it was hard manual labor as far as he was concerned. Not only that, it didn't fit the picture of the MacAllister family that King Chester had painted.

The MacAllisters, Brent thought, reaching into his mental memory bank, were highly respected in many areas of the professional careers arena. Their reputation was one of power, wealth, intelligence, indisputable honesty, and they also were known for giving back to their city by being involved as volunteers in various charitable activities. The name MacAllister had clout. They were upper-crust, movers and shakers.

But Alice was a waitress?

Oh, yes, curiouser and curiouser. And very intriguing was the lovely Ms. Alice. A mystery waiting to be solved. A puzzle, he'd dubbed it earlier, beckoning to him to piece it together. A delectable package that would be unwrapped very carefully, one layer at a time.

Brent frowned slightly as he pushed his salad away and slid a glance at Alice.

A mystery, a puzzle, a delectable package? he thought. He sure was getting poetic in his thirty-second year, which was very out of character for him.

Maybe…yes, this thought had merit…maybe his determination to learn all there was to know about Alice MacAllister was due to his having jet lag from the flight over from Wilshire. His tired brain was a tad fuzzy.

And maybe…but somehow he doubted it…his sexual attraction to Alice was a product of his fatigue, as well. When he'd held her hands as she stood so enticingly close to him after she'd fixed his tie, he had been consumed with desire so explosive, so hot, wild and burning, that he'd felt as if he were going up in flames.

There had been a crackling...something, a nearly palpable entity, weaving back and forth between them like nothing he'd ever experienced before.

Jet lag? No, forget that. It was something else, something more, something that needed to be explored and defined.

"Brent?" Trip said, bringing him from his rambling thoughts.

"Yes? What? Pardon me?" he asked.

"Did I wake you?" Trip said, smiling. "The waiter wants to know if you're finished with your salad. I realize it's a major decision in your life, but..."

Brent laughed. "Yes, I've had enough salad, thank you. The major decision I was facing was whether to eat those radishes or put them in a vase. Heavy stuff, so I'll just pass and have the plate removed to give my beleaguered brain a break."

"Oh, okay," Trip said, unable to keep from laughing as the waiter picked up Brent's salad plate.

Wonder of wonders, she thought. She was having a good time, was actually enjoying herself, having fun.

Because of Brent Bardow.

He was just so…so real. He was a member of a royal family, was the nephew of the king and cousin to the heir to the throne, yet he wasn't acting pompous or putting on airs. He obviously had a comfortable and loving relationship with his parents. Brent had a quick wit and caused her to laugh right out loud, something she didn't do easily.

Yes, she liked Brent Bardow.

But…

Trip smiled at the waiter as he placed a plate in front of her that held a fluffy baked potato smothered in butter, French green beans with slivers of almonds and a succulent slice of roast beef.

But, she thought, resuming her train of thought, she mustn't forget that Brent was capable of rendering her speechless, hardly able to breathe, when he pinned her in place with those incredible blue eyes of his.

She had to remember how off kilter she'd felt as the heat of instantaneous desire had whipped throughout her. When she'd stood close, so close, to him, it had felt like a fire raging out of control.

She must keep—front-row center in her mind— the fact that Brent was dangerous, a threat to her focus, should she succumb to his blatant sexuality and masculinity. Nothing, no one, would be allowed to keep her from accomplishing what she was setting out to do.

She could enjoy Brent's company while he was in Ventura if he chose to spend time with her, but she would keep him at arm's length, both physically and emotionally.

No problem. She had it all figured out.

"Very good," Trip said, nodding decisively.

"How do you know?" Brent said. "You haven't tasted anything on your plate yet."

Trip was saved from replying by King Chester getting to his feet.

"If I may have your attention for a moment, please," he said. "Your glasses are being filled with the newest and finest wine from Wilshire, the Renault-Bardow, which was created by my nephew, Brent. As you all know, it was while Devon was in this country marketing the wine that he met his Maggie. I hereby propose a toast to Maggie and Devon. May they have a long and happy life together and be blessed with the babies I've been waiting to bounce on my knee." King Chester raised his glass in the air. "To Maggie and Devon."

"Hear, hear," Robert MacAllister said.

Everyone at the table raised their glasses, then took a sip of the wine, which resulted in a buzz of compliments about the flavor as King Chester sat back down.

"You created this wine?" Trip said to Brent. "It's delicious. Very different. Special. Congratulations, Brent."

"Thank you," he said, touching his glass to hers. "It was several years in the making, but I finally accomplished what I set out to do."

"You were obviously focused on your goal, your dream."

Brent laughed. "I think it was closer to being possessed, like a mad scientist. I exhaust myself whenever I look back at the long hours I put in each day for all that time." He took another sip of the wine. "But it was worth it."

"Heartfelt dreams are worth that kind of sacrifice," Trip said quietly.

"True. Do you have a heartfelt dream, Alice?"

"You betcha," she said breezily, averting her gaze from his. "I'm going to get the owner of the Pop In Café to change the uniforms the waitresses have to wear even if I have to nag the man to the point of insanity."

"There you go. Good luck."

"Thank you very much," Trip said, then picked up her fork and began to eat.

That was it? Brent thought. That was her agenda

for the future? She didn't have some secret passion that would consume her, keep her separated from those around her who cared about her? Could that actually be fantastically true?

"Brent," Charlane Bardow said, "did the airlines call you back about that flight you wanted to be on tomorrow to return to the island?"

Trip's head snapped up and she stared at Brent.

He was leaving Ventura? she thought. Tomorrow? But he had just arrived here and…

"No," Brent said. "They're supposed to contact me if they get a last-minute cancellation but…" He turned his head to smile at Alice, then redirected his attention to his mother. "I believe I was a bit hasty in saying I would only stay the one night here."

"Oh?" Charlane and Byron Bardow, as well as Jillian and Forrest MacAllister, all said in unison, their gazes darting back and forth between Trip and Brent.

Trip felt a warm flush of embarrassment creep into her cheeks, and for the lack of anything better to do, drained her wineglass.

"Well, I…" Brent cleared his throat. "Witnessing Uncle Chester toasting Maggie and Devon with the Renault-Bardow wine makes me realize that I've earned a little time off from the vineyards, should have a vacation, of sorts. I'll call Peter and tell him to cover for me. He's a top-notch foreman, so... He can always contact me if there's a problem or..."

"You're babbling, dear," Charlane said. "We're delighted that you're staying on, considering I had to resort to motherly tears to get you to make this trip at all. You deserve to relax and enjoy yourself."

"Right," Brent said, cutting his meat. "Enough said on the subject."

Jillian and Forrest, and Charlane and Byron, exchanged smiling, speculative glances, but didn't say another word, per Brent's instructions. The noise level in the room increased again as everyone ate the delicious meal and carried on conversations around the table.

"You didn't want to come to Ventura?" Trip asked Brent.

"No."

"Why not?" she asked, frowning slightly.

"To quote you, Ms. MacAllister, it's old news, long story. There's something far more important on my mind at the moment."

"Which is?"

Brent smiled. "Would you pass the salt, please?"

Chapter Two

By the time the dessert of red raspberries nestled in rich French vanilla custard was served, Trip mentally marveled at how the royal family and the MacAllister clan interacted as though they had known one another for years, rather than mere hours.

It wasn't just Brent. Maggie was marrying into a wonderful family, no doubt about it.

The conversations during the meal revealed that the visitors would stay in Ventura for two weeks, then Maggie and her parents would accompany the Renaults and Bardows on the return trip to prepare for the royal wedding. The remainder of the MacAllister family would travel to the island for the affair a month after that.

Two weeks, Trip mused, sliding a quick glance at Brent. It would appear, from the attention he'd shown her all evening, that Brent intended to see more of her while he was in town.

Two weeks. She could handle that. If Brent did seek her out, she was perfectly capable of enjoying his no-strings-attached company. She would not become another of what was probably a long list of women who had succumbed to his good looks, charm and sensual masculinity, topped off by those incredible blue eyes.

And a good time was had by all, Trip thought, rather smugly, then took a bite of the delicious dessert.

"What do you think? Do you want to go with us, Brent?" Charlane said.

"No, thanks," he said. "I've been there a couple of times, so I'll pass."

Oh, dear, Trip thought, she'd been so busy carrying on a conversation with herself that she had no idea what everyone was talking about.

"Are you going to tag along on the great adventure?" Brent asked Alice.

"I...um...can't. I haven't been working at the

café long enough to have any vacation days on the books. So, I... No, I won't be going to...nope."

"Our triplets have been to Disneyland more times than I can count," Forrest said.

Oh. Disneyland, Trip thought. Thank you, Dad, for clearing that up.

"There was a string of years while they were young girls," Forrest continued, "that they'd put their three heads together and decide that was where they wanted to go for their birthday. I used to have nightmares about spinning teacups."

"Triplets?" Brent said, raising his eyebrows, then looking at Alice. "You're one of a set of triplets? I didn't know that." He glanced at Jessica and Emily. "Well, sure, I can see it now. I knew you three resembled one another but...I'll be darned. You are identical triplets."

"It's hard to tell," Emily said, "because I weigh far more than Jessica and Trip. Do note, though, family, that I did not have dessert, nor did I put sour cream on my potato. I am on a very serious diet and ten pounds are already history."

"Well, good for you, Emily," Charlane said. "I shouldn't have eaten my raspberries and custard, either, because I probably gained a pound just looking at it, let alone gobbling it up." She sighed. "I ate every delicious bite. Oh, shame on me."

"This is a special occasion, darling," Byron Bardow said, smiling warmly at his wife. "Besides, I'd love you no matter what you weighed."

"Well, bless your heart." Charlane laughed. "In that case, maybe I'll ask for another serving of dessert. No, no, I'll hold myself back."

"Maggie," her mother, Jenny, said to the bride-to-be, "have you given fair warning to Devon that twins and triplets run in our family in vast numbers?"

"She has," Devon said, nodding. "When it comes to babies…the more the merrier."

"Easy for you to say, Devon." Jillian laughed. "I lugged around triplets for nine months. It's no picnic, believe me. I completely forgot what my feet looked like. Grim."

"You were gorgeous," Forrest said, giving his wife a quick kiss on the lips. "I predicted you would have triplet girls and…bingo…you did. That was way back when I was the baby-bet champion of this family. Man, I was good, unbeatable for a very long time." He chuckled and shook his head. "It's hard to believe how many years have passed since then. But we're getting off the subject. The issue at hand is who wants to travel down the coast to Disneyland?"

Everyone suddenly seemed to start talking at once about the proposed journey.

"You've been to Disneyland?" Trip asked Brent.

He nodded. "Yep. I attended college at UCLA. Unlike Devon, this is not my first time in the United States. I lived here while I got my degrees in agriculture and viticulture, then returned home to the Island of Wilshire where I intend to live out my days messin' around with my grapes."

"Messin' around with your grapes?" Trip said, with a burst of laughter. "That's pretty high-tech jargon you're using there, Mr. Bardow."

"And you, Ms. MacAllister," he said, lowering his voice so only she could hear, "have the most beautiful laughter I have ever heard. It's like wind chimes. It would fill the cloudiest day with sunshine, and it makes those gorgeous brown eyes of yours actually sparkle with merriment. I do...oh, yes, I do like the sound of your laughter."

"Oh, well thank you," Trip said. "No one has ever commented on it before. I guess I've never given it any thought, either. Laughter is laughter."

"Wrong. Some people force it, make it part of a phony facade. Some people laugh too loud because they're attempting to become the center of attention. Yours is just right."

"Are you doing your own version of the three bears?" Trip said, smiling.

"Nope. You can't be Goldilocks, you're already Alice in Wonderland. I think your cousin Maggie is Cinderella because she's going to marry the prince. I wonder who else is in this room?" He glanced around. "Ah, I have it. Your sister Emily is Sleeping Beauty. She said she was on a serious diet, so she'll eventually wake up the woman within her and be who she really is and wants to be."

"You're very perceptive, very...sensitive," Trip said. "I doubt that anyone could put anything over on you that you didn't pick up on right off the bat."

"Don't bet the farm on that one," Brent said, a slight edge to his voice. "I'd like to think that I've learned how to read people correctly due to... I'll sure as hell give it my best shot now, believe me." He paused. "So! What's your favorite thing at Disneyland, Alice?"

"The boat ride through the It's a Small World castle," she said. Secrets. Brent Bardow had more than his share of secrets. "And you?"

"Ears."

"Pardon me?"

Brent laughed. "The best part is buying one of those Mickey Mouse hats and walking around all day with those dynamite ears perched on the top of my head. Hey, we're talking way cool here.''

"You're crazy,'' Trip said, her laughter mingling with Brent's. "You're fun and funny, and totally nuts."

"You would be, too, if you spent your life talking to grapes."

"But you love your work *and* the Island of Wilshire. Right?"

"Yes. Yes, I truly do," he said, nodding. "You'll see how beautiful Wilshire is when you come for the wedding. Who knows? Maybe you won't want to leave…ever."

"Oh, I couldn't stay on the island," Trip said, attempting to ignore the funny little two-step her heart suddenly executed.

"Why not?" Brent said, raising his eyebrows.

"I don't know diddly about grapes."

"Well, I'd just have to teach you all I know about—" Brent looked directly into Alice's eyes "—grapes."

"That might be—" Trip started, unable to tear her gaze from Brent's "—interesting."

As though pulled by invisible threads, Brent leaned closer to Alice, his gaze shifting to her slightly parted lips.

The sound of her grandfather clearing his throat

caused Trip to jerk. She glanced around and felt an instant flush on her cheeks as she saw that everyone at the table was staring at her and Brent. She looked at her grandfather, who winked at her, then got to his feet.

"It's been a marvelous evening," he said, "but it's time for Margaret and me to head for home and our soft pillows. As the senior member of the MacAllister family, King Chester, let me say what a pleasure it has been to get to know you and yours. We're all very pleased that you'll be staying in Ventura for a while."

"I'll second that," Forrest said, then pushed back his chair. "Ready to go, Jillian?" He rose, then looked across the table. "Trip, is your car still being repaired? Do you need a ride home?"

"Yes, my poor clunker is being held captive by the mechanic. I came here in a taxi, and I'll just take another one home, Dad. My place is miles out of your way."

"That's no problem," Forrest said. "Your mother and I will see you safely home."

"Forrest," Jillian said, laughing as she got to her feet, "you're slipping into your protective daddy mode. The night is young to the next generation in this room. Trip might not be ready to end the evening."

"She's not," Brent said quickly, then looked at Alice. "Are you? Would you like to go dancing?"

Trip frowned. "Dancing? Goodness, I haven't danced since I was in high school."

"It's like riding a bike. It will all come back to you when the music starts. Are you game, Alice?"

"Oh, well…" she said. No, she had to get up very early to be at work for the breakfast crowd at the café. The sensible thing to do was to accept her father's offer of a ride and get a solid night's sleep. She was not, however, in a particularly sensible mood at the moment. Brent was making her feel so alive, young and carefree, and… "Yes, I'd like to go dancing, very much."

"Who wants to join us?" Brent said, sweeping his gaze over the group.

No one accepted the invitation due to a host of excuses.

Brent shrugged. "Guess it's just the two of us, Alice in Wonderland."

"Don't you have to work in the morning, Trip?" Forrest said.

"Say good-night, Forrest," Jillian said, poking him in the ribs with her elbow. "That's your line. Good night, everyone."

Forrest sighed. "You're right. I'm sorry. Old

habits just don't dissolve that easily. Good night, everyone. This was a terrific evening.''

A flurry of farewell hugs were exchanged by all, and ten minutes later Trip and Brent were in a taxi headed for a popular nightclub.

"I've got it," Brent said, snapping his fingers. "You use the nickname Trip because you like being a triplet. Right?"

"Not exactly," Trip said, frowning as she shook her head. "I detested being a triplet when I was growing up, having people ask which one I was. When I was eight or nine years old, I announced that people might as well just call me Trip because they didn't view me as an individual but one of an interchangeable set. The name stuck. Everyone except my grandfather still calls me Trip."

"Oh," Brent said, nodding. "Being a triplet wasn't fun and games, huh?"

"Not for me," Trip said quietly. "It never seemed to bother Emily and Jessica, but… So! You solved that mystery. You owe me one."

"One what?"

"Answer to an unsolved mystery," Trip said. "Why didn't you want to make the trip? And why did you plan to only stay long enough to attend the dinner tonight?"

Brent stared out the side window of the taxi for a long moment, then shifted his gaze back to Alice.

"Let's just say that I don't have particularly fond memories of my years here in the States and I didn't feel like reliving them." He paused. "But now I've met you, I'm looking forward to my stay in Ventura. I hope you'll agree to spend time with me while I'm here, Alice. I really do."

"I'd like that, but I don't think you answered my questions."

"I was close enough. And right on time because we're here. Ready to rock and roll, or hip-hop or whatever they call this stuff these days."

"Mmm," Trip said absently. Brent had just done some very fancy verbal footwork. What had happened to him during the years he'd attended college in this country? Oh, yes, the man definitely had secrets.

But then, she thought, as Brent assisted her from the cab, so did she.

Due to it being a work night, the club wasn't crowded and Trip and Brent had their choice of several tables edging a large dance floor. A waitress appeared wearing a short fringed skirt, a vest over a tube top, boots and a white Stetson perched jauntily on her head.

"It's country-western night," she said, smiling,

"in case you didn't figure that out already." She laughed. "Y'all. What can I get you?"

Both Trip and Brent ordered soft drinks.

"Got it," the waitress said. "Oops. Almost forgot to say 'y'all.' On hip-hop night I call everyone dude. Drives me nuts. Back in a few."

"Oh, dear," Trip said, looking at the people who were dancing. "They're doing that western thing... you know, the two-step or whatever it is. I'm definitely out of my league here."

Brent shrugged. "We'll just wait for a slow song and they won't know we don't have a clue as to how to do line dancing, or whatever." He paused. "You moved back to Ventura over the holidays. Where were you living before you returned home?"

"San Francisco. I was there for three years. Before that? Here, there and everywhere."

"Do I detect a wanderlust spirit?" Brent said, frowning slightly.

"No, not really. I'm back in Ventura to stay...I hope."

The waitress returned with their drinks, told them to give a shout, y'all, if they wanted refills, then hurried off.

"You *hope* to stay in Ventura?" Brent said. "It's your choice to make, isn't it?"

Trip sighed, then poked at the ice in her glass with the straw.

"It's rather complicated, Brent," she said, looking at an ice cube bob up and down. "I'd rather not discuss it, if you don't mind. Let's just say that I'm waiting to discover if the old cliché, you can't go home again, is true, and leave it at that."

"Sure. Okay. Well, one thing is a given. You have a great family. I imagine they're delighted that you decided to move back here."

Trip shrugged as she continued to dunk the ice cube.

"Aren't they?" Brent said, leaning slightly toward her. "Alice?"

Trip met Brent's gaze. "Brent, don't push. Please. I said I didn't want to talk about this."

"Hey, I'm sorry," he said, covering her free hand with his on the top of the table. "I just…well, I want to get to know you better." He rolled his eyes heavenward. "Oh, man, I can't believe I said that. Corny to the max. The thing is, it's true. I *do* want to understand who you are, what makes you tick, because I…I like you, Alice." He smiled. "Y'all."

"I like you, too, but… The band just started a slow song," she said. "Vince Gill's 'Look at Us.' Do you know the words? It's beautiful."

"I don't think I've ever heard it."

"It's about a man marveling at how much he still loves his wife. Even though they've been together such a long time. He still sees her as being pretty as a picture. In this sad age of married today, divorced tomorrow, I think this song is so lovely, so meaningful and romantic."

"Then let's dance to it."

"I'd like that."

Trip walked in front of Brent to the dance floor, then turned and moved into his arms. He nestled her against him as they swayed to the music, holding her not too tightly, not too far away, but just right.

She was dancing with a magnificent man, Trip thought dreamily. Oh, he felt so good, so strong and powerful, yet had such a gentle aura. He smelled good, too, like fresh air and soap and something that was just him, the man, Brent.

"Ah, Alice," Brent said quietly, "look at us."

Trip tilted her head back to gaze into the depths of Brent's blue eyes and smiled at him. In the next instant her smile faded as she saw raw desire change the hue of Brent's eyes to a smoky gray at the same moment she felt the heat of her own desire begin to pulse low within her.

Oh, yes, she thought, look at us. They wanted

each other, wanted to make love for hours and hours. It didn't seem to matter that they'd just met...the want, the need, the fire within them was there, burning hotter with every beat of their hearts.

The beautiful song ended, and the band launched into a loud, wild version of "Boot Scootin' Boogie." As the other dancers on the floor whirled and twirled around them, Trip and Brent continued to dance slowly, oblivious to their surroundings, as they gazed into each other's eyes.

Time lost meaning.

One song led to another, then yet another, and still they danced, hearing their own music and the words to "Look at Us" over and over again.

"Last call for drinks," someone yelled.

Trip and Brent were jerked from the misty, sensuous place they had floated to. They stumbled slightly, then stopped dancing. Brent slowly, and so reluctantly, released his hold on Alice.

"I..." Trip started, then averted her eyes from Brent's as she busied herself smoothing nonexistent wrinkles from the skirt of her dress. "I had no idea it was so late. I...I have to get up early in the morning for work and..."

"Alice," Brent said, his voice husky.

"Hmm?" she said, lifting her head slowly to meet his gaze.

"There is something totally terrifying happening between us."

Trip's eyes widened. "Totally terrifying? Dangerous and...oh, thank goodness. This is wonderful."

"Huh?" Brent said, frowning. "Come on, let's go back to the table where we can discuss this privately before they toss us out of here and close for the night."

When they were seated again, Trip smiled at Brent.

"Okay," he said. "You have the floor. What's wonderful about this totally terrifying whatever it is?"

"That fact that we're on the same wavelength, Brent. The same page, as the modern jargon goes. Oh, don't you see? We're very aware of the incredible sexual attraction between us. It's...it's like nothing *I've* ever experienced before, that's for sure. But since we both feel it's a tad terrifying, dangerous, even overwhelming at times, we can decide...together...what we want to do about it, knowing that neither of us can be hurt because it's all temporary and—"

"Hold it," Brent said, raising one hand. "You're making sense, but I'd like to clarify one thing you said. This is more than just sexual attraction. That term edges toward lust, Alice, and that is very tacky. There are emotions involved here, too, caring, wanting to know who the other person is, how we feel about things, and...understand? Are you with me here?''

Trip nodded slowly. ''Yes, all right, I'll go with that. Fine. But my point is, whatever it is that's throwing us so off kilter isn't totally terrifying or dangerous because we both know it's there.

''We also know that you're only in Ventura for two weeks, then later I'll be on the Island of Wilshire for the wedding, and...and that will be that. We have the data, the facts, Brent. There is absolutely no chance of either of us being hurt, or one of us having our heart smashed to smithereens, because we're dealing up-front with how things stand.''

Brent stared into space. ''Oh.''

''That's it?'' Trip said. ''I just delivered one of the longest speeches of my entire life, and all you have to say in response is...oh?''

''I'm digesting your dissertation,'' he said, looking at her again. ''I have jet lag, remember? My brain isn't operating at full power.'' He leaned back in his chair and folded his arms across his chest. ''So, what you're saying...bottom line...is that whatever decisions we make as consenting adults regarding what we do as…as consenting adults isn't risky business because we're consenting adults who have analyzed the damn thing to death.''

"What are you getting so crabby about? And don't say consenting adults again, because it's getting on my nerves.''

Brent laughed and moved forward again. "I'm a consenting adult who is very rattled at the moment.'' He paused. "Seriously, I do understand what you're saying and it's very valid. A little cold, a little clinical, but it has merit.''

"It certainly does.''

"Head 'em up and move 'em out,'' the bartender yelled. "Y'all.''

Brent got to his feet and extended one hand to Alice. "We're outta here.''

Trip placed her hand in Brent's and allowed him to draw her up and close to him.

"Will you have dinner with me tomorrow night?'' he said, then glanced at his watch. "Well, technically it's already tomorrow, but…seven o'clock?''

"I…yes, I'd like that. Since you'll have a taxi waiting, I'll be in the lobby to my building at seven.''

Brent nodded and they started toward the door of the club with the other people who were leaving.

Outside a line formed as waiting taxis collected fares and drove away. When it was their turn, Brent reached for the handle of the back door of the vehicle, then hesitated.

"What's wrong?" Trip said.

"This cab has tinted windows that are acting almost like mirrors."

"That's nice. Open the door. It's chilly out here in my slip."

"In a second," Brent said, encircling her waist with one arm and pulling her close to his side. He cocked his head toward their reflection in the window of the door. "Look at us, Alice in Wonderland."

Chapter Three

Trip yawned as she hung her sweater on the designated hook in the rear of the kitchen of the Pop In Café early the next morning. Her hand lingering on the sweater, she stared into space, a soft smile forming on her lips as the lilting melody of the song "Look at Us" floated dreamily through her mind.

Last night, she mused, had been...well, heavenly. She'd had such a marvelous time with Brent, had thoroughly enjoyed the entire evening. She'd even been more relaxed while in the company of her huge family.

And dancing with Brent? Oh, gracious, there

were hardly words to describe how feminine, cherished and desired she'd felt, while held in Brent's embrace. The sensual mist that had encased them in their private world had been like nothing she'd experienced before.

It had taken every bit of her willpower to firmly state that Brent was to remain in the taxi when it stopped in front of her apartment building. She'd blithered on about how late it was, how early she had to get up, how she was perfectly safe going inside alone because there was a security guard on duty at a desk in the lobby. So, thank you, Brent, for a lovely time and...

And then he'd kissed her.

Trip sighed.

That kiss, she thought, had been incredible. Brent had slid his hand to the nape of her neck, lowered his head and claimed her lips with his...right there in the taxi for anyone who cared to look to be a witness. Mmm. That kiss. Heat had coursed through her with such intensity she was convinced that her bones were dissolving and she'd just slither into a puddle on the sidewalk when she attempted to walk to the door of the building.

That kiss had caused her to desire Brent Bardow to the point that she had instant visions of making sweet, slow love with him through the remaining hours of the night. She'd managed, somehow, to sort of slide out of the cab, dash across the sidewalk and into the lobby.

Oh, my, that kiss had been so…

"Say goodbye to your sweater, Alice," a voice said. "There are hungry customers in your station."

Trip jerked and returned to the reality of the shabby little café, pulling her hand quickly away from the silly sweater.

"Hi, Hilda," she said to a plump woman in her forties who was wearing the same bright pink uniform Trip was. "I was daydreaming, I guess. Sorry."

Hilda laughed. "You were hanging on to that sweater like it was an adult form of a security blanket."

"I just forgot to let go of it," Trip said, smiling. "I'm a tad tired this morning. Why does this place have to start serving breakfast at 6 a.m.?"

"Because that's when people get hungry," a man said, then turned bacon on a griddle. "You ladies ready to earn the big bucks I pay you?"

"Big bucks?" Hilda said with a hoot of laughter. "You're so full of bull, Poppy. This must be a labor of love on our part, because we sure aren't doing it for the money, you tightfisted bum."

Poppy, an extremely skinny man in his sixties,

chuckled. "Labor of love? That I know to be the truth. The ladies have been after my body since I hit puberty. What can I say? I'm irresistible. But instead of ravishing me, go wait on the customers. Shoo."

"Going, going, going," Trip said, then hurried across the room and through the swinging doors leading to the outer area of the café.

She zoomed past the counter where several men were sitting on stools covered in red leather, and headed for the booths she was in charge of. Then she stopped so quickly she teetered, her eyes widening.

"Brent?" she said, walking forward slowly. She stopped next to the booth where he was sitting. "What...what are you doing here?"

"Having breakfast," he said, smiling up at her.

"Here?" Trip said incredulously.

"Why not?" he said, lifting one shoulder in a shrug. He retrieved the plastic-covered menu from behind the metal napkin holder. "What's good?"

"I have no idea," she said, still staring at him. "I've only eaten the pie, remember? I...you really want to have breakfast...here?"

"What I really want," he said quietly, meeting her gaze, "is to say good morning to you, see you, hear your laughter, share another kiss with you."

"Shh." Trip glanced quickly around. "Go back to the breakfast thing. Coffee?"

Brent nodded. "And a number three, with the eggs over easy."

"Right," Trip said, then turned and rushed away.

Alice was flustered, Brent thought, watching her. He was obviously the last person she expected to find in this crummy place this morning.

But…so, okay, he'd admit it to himself. He just didn't want to have to wait until their dinner date tonight to see Alice MacAllister. The image of her in his mind had caused him to toss and turn through the few remaining hours of the night when he'd returned to his hotel. The remembrance of the kiss…

That kiss, Brent mused, looking out the grimy window of the café. That kiss he'd shared with Alice in the cab had been sensational. And *shared* was an important word there, because Alice had returned his kiss in total abandon. Sensational. Man, oh, man, how he'd wanted her, wanted to make love with her for hours, wanted…

Brent shifted in the booth as heat rocketed through his body and looked up to see Alice approaching with a coffeepot and a mug. She plunked the mug on the table and began to fill it.

"I would have thought you'd be sleeping. I mean, you were suffering from jet lag, then we were out late dancing and... You should have done that, you know. Slept. Not gotten up at the crack of dawn and—"

"Alice..." Brent said.

"—and come to this place for breakfast when you could have had room service in your hotel, I assume, and rested because—"

"Alice," Brent said, grabbing a handful of napkins out of the holder, "the mug is overflowing."

"Oh!" she said. "Oh, dear me, I'm so sorry. I wasn't paying attention and...I'll get you a clean mug and wipe up the table and..."

"Am I upsetting you by being here?" Brent said, raising his eyebrows.

"Of course, you are, you dolt. I mean, for Pete's sake, members of royal families don't eat in this dump. And I was just thinking about you, and then here you are, and it's like I conjured you up by mentally dwelling on the kiss and the dancing to our song, and the..." She smacked her free hand against her forehead. "I can't believe I just said all that." She sighed. "Okay, fine. I'm totally mortified. I'll go get your number three, and I hope it tastes terrible."

"*Our* song? Hey, I like that. It's kind of teenage corny, but...I really like that. We have a special song that is ours. And I'm delighted to hear that you were thinking about me, the dancing, the kiss. We're still on the same wavelength the morning after.''

"This is not a morning after," Trip whispered, leaning toward him. "You're making it sound as though we... What I mean is... You know."

"Alice," Poppy yelled through the pass-through window to the kitchen. "You want this number three, or what?"

Trip glared at Brent, spun around and stomped off, a shiver slithering down her spine as she heard his throaty chuckle behind her.

"Who's the hunk of stuff?" Hilda said as Trip retrieved Brent's breakfast plate from the ledge.

"A member of the royal family of the Island of Wilshire. He's the cousin to the prince, who is the heir to the throne."

"Oh, okay," Hilda said, laughing. "Can I be Madonna? No, wait. I'll be Julia Roberts because she's got that cute guy, what's his name. Who are you this morning?"

"Me? Oh, what the heck. If you can't beat 'em, join 'em. I, my dear Hilda, am Alice in Wonderland."

Hours later, refreshed from a nap and a long soak in a bubble bath, Trip smoothed the waistband of a red string sweater over her navy blue slacks.

At the café that morning, Brent had said he was hungry for some good ole U.S.A. pizza and they'd agreed that they would go to a pizza place for dinner. He'd then declared that his breakfast was delicious, an announcement that had caused her eyes to widen in surprise.

Trip walked from behind the decorative screens that created the sleeping area of her loft, then stopped, sweeping her gaze over the large expanse.

A chill coursed through her, and she wrapped her arms around her elbows.

No, she thought. She was not emotionally prepared, just not ready, for anyone in her family to see this. And she most definitely didn't intend to invite Brent Bardow to enter her sanctum.

Trip sank onto the puffy sofa and sighed as she leaned her head on the top and stared at the ceiling.

But, she thought, how many excuses could she come up with as to why Brent should bid her adieu out in the hall?

How many times did she *wish* to end an evening with the lingering feel of Brent's lips on hers, just that kiss and nothing more? How many times? None. She wanted Brent. She wanted to make love with him, hold and kiss, touch and taste him.

"You're a wanton woman, Trip MacAllister," she said, raising her head.

But she didn't care how brazen and out of character her passion for Brent was. It was there, it was real, and it made her feel alive and vital, acutely aware of her womanliness.

She and Brent were on measured, borrowed time, with a date clearly marked on the calendar saying when he would return home. Even though she'd travel to the island a month after that, her stay there would be short, and it might even be impossible to escape from the families and be alone with each other.

She'd never been in a situation like this before, Trip mused. She'd never engaged in an affair that would be over because one of the participants flew off to the other side of the world.

She was usually the one in the few—very few—relationships she'd engaged in in the past to end things when they became too serious, when she began to feel pressured, smothered, was having more asked of her than she was willing, able to give.

Actually, there was nothing *ordinary* about this…this whatever it was…with Brent, Trip thought, getting to her feet. From the very moment she'd seen him fumbling with his tie, it was as though everything was magnified and moving at fast forward. So, it stood to reason that her determination to make love with him, a man she'd known such a short length of time, was out of the ordinary as well. That made sense. It really did.

"Fine," Trip said, planting her hands on her hips. "I want to make love with Brent, but I can't invite him into my home, and I really don't want to share that intimate act with him out in the hall."

But...but she wasn't ready to have him come through that door and see...

Trip glanced quickly at her watch, her mind racing. She ran to the door, then down the hall to the next one, knocking loudly when she arrived. The door was opened by a nice-looking man in his mid-thirties.

"Hey, Trip," he said, "what's doin'?"

"I'm about to ask you for a really big favor, Denny," she said. "I need your muscles and some space in your loft to stash some stuff...now. I'm in a major rush."

"May I ask why?" Denny said.

"No."

"Got it." Denny shrugged. "Okay, whatever. Let's do it."

"Oh, thank you," Trip said, grabbing his arm and hauling him forward. "Thank you, Denny."

Trip was waiting for Brent in the lobby of the building as planned and went outside when she saw him start to get out of a taxi that had arrived at the curb.

"I'm ready to go," she said, as Brent rose to stand in front of her. "Pizza. Mmm. I'm starving, too."

"Well, okay," he said, frowning slightly, "but I would have come in and gotten you at your apartment, you know." He smiled. "My mother would give me a stern lecture on my gentlemanly manners because I didn't collect you at the door to your home."

"We won't tell her," Trip said, matching his smile. "Your mother is so nice. She's fun and—"

"Trip," a voice called, causing Trip and Brent to turn in the direction the sound had come from.

Bobby MacAllister came trotting down the street, stopped in front of them and took a much-needed breath.

"Whew, I'm sure out of shape," he said. "Okay, I can breathe again. Look, Trip, I know you told the family that we shouldn't just drop by your new place unannounced, but this is an emergency. Besides, you're not *in* your place, you're standing on the sidewalk *outside* your place, so..."

"Bobby, what's wrong? What's the emergency?"

"Oh. Diane went to the doctor today and he said the baby could come any time now. So, I went out and rented cell phones for everyone in the family who doesn't have one so I can contact you when the big event happens.'' He extended one hand toward Trip. ''Here's your phone. Man, I'm a wreck. I am coming unglued. Diane is so calm it's driving me crazy. She just pats her stomach and tells the kid to come on out whenever it's ready. I swear, Trip, I'm not going to survive this.''

Trip took the cell phone and put it in her purse. ''This is a marvelous idea, Bobby. I'm…I'm very touched that you thought of me when you…thank you.''

''Hey, sweet cousin,'' he said, ''you're a very important part of this family. We've really missed having you with us all these years, and Diane and I hope you'll stay on in Ventura and be a spoil-you-rotten auntie-type person to our child. Nobody is torked at you about the past. This is now. Okay?''

''Yes,'' Trip said quietly. ''I'm struggling with that theory, but I'm trying to fit in, Bobby. Tell Diane I'm thinking of her. I'll be waiting for this phone to ring and…my goodness, this is exciting. This is the first time I'll be going to the hospital for the birth of one of the MacAllister babies.''

''Yep. Nice to see you again, Brent. For the record, I can't say I'm surprised you're with Trip. That won't be a big news flash to anyone in the family after last night at the restaurant and... Hey, I don't have time to chat. I've got phones to deliver, then I gotta get home and have Diane hold my hand so I'll get it together. Bye.''

"Bye, Bobby,'' Trip called, as her cousin sprinted off down the sidewalk in the direction he'd come from.

"You folks going someplace, or what?'' the taxi driver yelled.

"Oops,'' Trip said, then slid onto the back seat of the cab. She leaned forward and gave the driver the address of the restaurant as Brent settled next to her and pulled the door closed.

"Wasn't Bobby cute? Talk about a flustered daddy-to-be.''

"Mmm,'' Brent said.

"Bobby has had months to prepare for the arrival of the baby and now he's a blithering idiot. I think that's so adorable.''

"Mmm.''

"I wonder if it's a girl or a boy?'' Trip rambled on. "If it was me, I wouldn't care either way if it was healthy and... But I don't envision myself getting married and having babies, so that's a moot point. Bobby and Diane have a long list of possible names for their firstborn. Some were very strange. I wonder what they'll—''

"Alice," Brent said quietly.

Trip turned to look at Brent questioningly. "Yes, Brent?"

"Could we back up here a bit to some of the things your cousin said?" he said. "Like...your family is not to drop by your new place. No one is holding a grudge about the past. They all hope you'll stay on in Ventura, but apparently they're not convinced you will." Brent paused. "Let's toss in why you don't see yourself marrying and having babies, too, while we're at it."

A flash of anger coursed through Trip, then kept right on going and disappeared, leaving her feeling very vulnerable and exposed. Her shoulders slumped and she sighed.

"I was hoping you wouldn't pick up on all of that," she said, not looking at Brent as she fiddled with the clasp on her purse. "I *could* say it's none of your business."

"Yes, you could," Brent said, nodding, "but that sure would build a high wall between us, Alice, that you'd be hiding behind. Getting to know each other better would stop right here and now. That's not good. Not good at all. But, well, it's up to you as to whether you wish to share more of who you are with me. I can't force you to do it."

"Pizza," the taxi driver said, coming to a

screeching halt. "Hey, buddy, all women have secrets. You're better off not knowing what they are the majority of the time, because then you're supposed to automatically know how to deal with their feminine person, or whatever the hell they call it."

Brent leaned forward and gave the man a bill. "Keep the change."

"The advice was free," the man said. "Thanks for the nice tip, though. Enjoy your pizza, folks."

Right, Trip thought dryly, as Brent assisted her out of the vehicle. There was now a bowling ball in her stomach and no room left for any pizza. Two more minutes and Bobby would have missed catching her in front of her building and Brent wouldn't have heard her cousin chattering like a magpie. Darn, darn, darn.

The restaurant was fairly crowded, but Trip and Brent found an empty booth, agreed on the toppings for their pizza, then Brent went to place their order. He returned with a pitcher of cola, sat down opposite Alice and filled their glasses.

"Here's to—" he said, lifting his glass "—sharing and caring."

Trip stared at Brent's raised glass, at her own that she hadn't touched, then back at Brent's.

"All right," she said, her voice not quite steady.

She lifted her glass and clinked it against Brent's. "To sharing and caring."

They each took a sip of the cold, sweet drink, then set their glasses on the wooden table. Brent leaned back and spread his arms along the top of the leather booth.

She didn't *have* to tell Brent Bardow anything she chose to keep to herself, Trip thought, frowning slightly as she met his gaze. This wasn't a long-standing relationship with a hoped-for future together that would crumble into dust from the weight of secrets kept. This was a very short-term whatever it was, that had a beginning, middle and an ending already marked on the calendar.

There was no reason to bare her soul to Brent.

But yet...

She wanted to.

She didn't like the image in her mind of the wall between her and Brent that he had spoken of. She already had a barrier between herself and her family that was proving difficult to demolish. She had, in fact, kept an emotional distance from everyone she'd met since she'd left home years before. That's how she conducted her life, which meant she would never fall in love, marry, have babies, because it was too late to change who she was.

But if she lowered that barrier just a tad, answered just some of Brent's questions, it would be a...yes, a safe way to sort of practice at least peeking over the wall she'd erected around herself. Safe because what she had with Brent was temporary. It might enable her to make more positive overtures toward her family.

As far as stepping from behind the wall completely to enable her to fall in love? No. She'd be kidding herself if she thought she could ever do that. It was just too big, too frightening. No.

"Alice?" Brent said quietly.

"What?" She took a deep breath and let it out slowly. "Yes, all right. It's not all that complicated, Brent. I told you that I didn't like being one of the MacAllister triplets, and I did a bang-up job of rebelling against that role when I was a teenager.

"Jessica and Emily were excellent students, so I slacked off and just squeaked by as far as my grades went. They had oodles of friends, so I was a loner, kept to myself. They enjoyed nice clothes, so I wore funky junk from used-clothing stores. They obeyed every rule our parents had set in place, so I broke them all, like coming in later than our curfew. Nice kid, huh?"

Brent lifted one shoulder in a shrug. "You were establishing your own identity."

"In spades," Trip said. "I left home right after

high school graduation, refused to even talk about going to college. Not me, not the rebel. I went to New York and pursued... Well, anyway, I lived in New York City for several years, then went to Colorado, then on to San Francisco. I never told my family when I'd be home, I'd just show up from time to time. I...I hurt some wonderful people very, very much by the way I conducted myself.''

"But now you've come home."

Trip nodded. "I'd like to think I've finally matured to the point that I realize that what I did was wrong. I've missed my family and want to be a part of the MacAllister clan...but it might very well be too late."

Brent leaned forward and folded his arms on the top of the table.

"I find that hard to believe after meeting your family. They're warm, honest, open. I heard what Bobby said. No one is dwelling on the past."

"That may be true, but they're tense around me, afraid they might say something to upset me, cause me to pack it up and leave town again. I find it hard to relax around them, too. It's been so many years and... I don't know. I guess maybe it *is* complicated."

"Why don't you want them to drop by your apartment when they're in your neighborhood? Casual visits like that are often more comfortable than scheduled gatherings.''

''No,'' Trip said quickly. ''What I mean is, I'm not used to that, and the thought of it makes me edgy. I don't want to open my door and find a MacAllister standing there out of the blue. No.''

''I see,'' Brent said, nodding slowly. ''I guess. Okay, go on to the part about why you'll never marry and have kids.''

''It should be clear to you by what I've just explained. If I am struggling to connect with a group of people who love me unconditionally, it's far too late to let down my guard entirely, not protect myself in any manner, which is what is required to be an equal partner in a loving relationship, a marriage. I just wouldn't be able to give enough of myself to another person, risk that much.''

''But…'' Brent started, then cocked his head to one side. ''That's our number for the pizza. I'll be right back, Alice.''

Trip nodded, then Brent started to slide out of the booth. He stopped and looked directly into Alice's eyes.

''I think you're giving up on yourself too easily,'' he said. ''You know, saying you can't change enough to be an equal partner in a relationship and what have you. You should give yourself credit for what you just did here...with me.''

''What do you mean?''

''You talked to me, Alice, and I listened, really heard what you said,'' Brent said. ''You did the sharing and I did the caring. You can't beat that combination.''

Chapter Four

To Trip's heartfelt relief, when Brent returned to the table with the pizza, he launched into a discussion about a bestselling novel that was to be made into a movie. They engaged in a game of selecting what actors should play the roles of the various characters, which was rather silly but definitely fun.

When they left the restaurant, they stopped at an ice-cream store, bought two-scoop cones, then strolled along the sidewalk and window-shopped as they ate their creamy dessert. Brent pointed out that they both kept pushing the ice cream down so that the very last bite of the sugary cone would be filled.

"There's probably some scientific, psychological meaning behind that," Brent said, after popping the tip of the cone into his mouth. "Gives great insight into our personalities, which are, once again, on the same wavelength. Maybe I'll research it on the Internet."

"Oh, for heaven's sake," Trip laughed. "Emily used to bite the end off her cone and practically stand on her head to use it like a straw. I wonder what the shrinky-dinks would say about that?"

"Don't have a clue," Brent said, chuckling, "but I'm sure it's very important in regard to the identity of Emily's inner child. Speaking of child types, Emily has a son, right? He was sitting next to her at the dinner? Trevor. Yes, that was his name. He looked to be about twelve, or thirteen. Nice kid. I assume since there wasn't a dad on the scene at the party that Emily is divorced?"

"No," Trip said, tossing her napkin in a trash barrel as they walked past it. "Emily has never been married. She had Trevor when she was eighteen and has raised him alone."

"Whew, that's a tough job," Brent said, "especially when you take it on that young."

"The family was very supportive, there for her when she needed them," Trip said. "I honestly don't know what happened between her and

Mark...Trevor's father...because they had been together all through high school, then he suddenly left Ventura for college back east and...

"Well, the truth is I took off, too, so I never heard whatever explanation there was for their split. As time passed and I came home to visit, the opportunity to ask for details didn't present itself, nor did it seem to matter by then. I do know she named her baby Trevor *Mark* MacAllister, so she didn't end up despising Mark for leaving."

"Interesting."

"Trevor is a nice kid from what I gather," Trip continued, "although I guess he gives Emily a bad time about being overweight. He's at an age that having a...well, chubby mother embarrasses him, and he's rather vocal about the subject."

"Teenagers are not known for their diplomacy and tact at times. That statement doesn't include yours truly, of course. I was a prize, a peach of a teen, never gave my parents a moment of grief."

"Is your nose going to grow?" Trip asked, smiling up at him.

Brent laughed. "From here to Chicago. I was, shall we say, busy at that age. Poor ole Devon had to toe the line because he was the prince, the heir to the throne, but I was removed from that just enough to raise hell without lightning striking me dead.

"I got lots of lectures about behavior befitting a member of the royal family, but I wasn't under a microscope the way Devon was, and still is. Maggie will have to get used to that when she marries Devon and lives on the island, but I get the feeling she'll handle it just fine."

"I'm sure she will," Trip said, nodding. She glanced around. "Goodness, we've really trekked on and on here. We're only about a block from my apartment building. There won't be a need to hail a cab to see me home, Brent."

"Are you trying to tell me something, Alice? Like you're ready to end the evening?"

Trip stopped walking and met Brent's gaze, seeing the frown that knitted his brows.

"No," she said quietly, "I don't wish to end the evening yet, Brent." She paused and sighed. "I'm not very sophisticated, I guess. I don't know how to play the dating game, don't know all the rules and... You'll see me to my door, then I envision an awkward moment where I'm supposed to either say good-night, or invite you in. Right?"

Brent nodded. "That's how it generally goes."

"And if I invite you in on the pretext of having

coffee, I'm actually indicating that I want to…that I want to make love. Am I still right?''

"As a rule, yes. But if you invite me in and tell me it's for a cup of coffee and nothing more, I'll accept that. I won't like it, you understand, but I'll be a gentleman about it to the point of ad nauseam.''

Trip wrapped her hands around her elbows. "So, it's up to me, isn't it? To decide how this night will end. That is a tremendous responsibility, Brent, and…'' She shook her head.

"Hey,'' he said, gripping her shoulders. "It doesn't have to be like that, Alice. Everything about us is different, special, rare. We're not going to do that come-in-for-coffee nonsense. We're going to talk it through, discuss this like—''

"Consenting adults,'' Trip said, rolling her eyes heavenward. "Blak.''

Brent encircled Alice's shoulders with one arm and they started off down the sidewalk again.

"I've definitely overused that term,'' he said, smiling. "I won't say it again, I promise.'' He paused, his expression now serious. "Okay, we'll discuss this. I'll go first to make it easier for you.''

"Thank you,'' Trip said. A silent minute went by, then two, then three. "Brent?''

"I don't know how to do it,'' he said, raking his

free hand through his hair. "I'm programmed for the come-in-for-coffee bit.

"What am I supposed to do? Just open my mouth and tell you that I desire you more than any woman I've ever met? That I want you so badly I ache? That making love with you is never far from my thoughts, and I think we should sprint the remaining distance to your apartment so I can take you in my arms and…cripe. It's all true, but…damn it, Alice, help me out here."

Trip stopped walking and stared up at Brent with a rather astonished expression on her face.

"I don't believe this. You, Mr. Worldly and Wise, who probably has broken hearts across the globe, is admitting that you're feeling a tad awkward, rather jangled, shall we say, by this exchange we're having?"

Brent frowned. "I do not have a reputation for breaking hearts, my dear Ms. MacAllister. But as far as the rest of what you said…yeah, okay, I'm a little flustered, due to the fact that I've never taken part in a conversation like this one." He smiled. "But then, I've never met a woman like you before, either, so I guess that makes sense. Okay. I've bared my soul. The ball is now in your court."

Trip stared at Brent for another long moment, then she smiled. It was a lovely smile, a warm, womanly, I'm-glad-I'm-me-and-you-are-you smile. She reached up and framed Brent's face with her hands.

"I absolutely adore you, Brent Bardow," she said, the smile still firmly in place. "You're just so real, so down-to-earth. You take things that could become uncomfortable and complex and just smooth them out and make them seem so easy, simple, without diminishing their value. That's a gift, it truly is."

"Oh," Brent said. "You have such soft hands. I'll give you three years to get your dainty paws off my face."

Trip laughed in delight.

Brent had done it again, she marveled. He'd made her feel so young and carefree, happy and just plain old glad to be alive.

"I want to make love with you, Brent, very, very much. There. I said it out loud, just as you did. It feels right, the way it is meant to be. I'll have no regrets about taking this momentous step with you." She dropped her hands from his face and took off at a run. "You said we should sprint to my apartment," she yelled. "I'm leaving you in the dust."

"Hey!" Brent said, starting after her. "You

cheated, Alice. You're supposed to say ready, set, go.''

Brent's long legs covered the distance between him and Trip in short order. They entered the lobby of her building together, their laughter dancing through the air and accompanying them into the elevator.

A few minutes later, Brent was sweeping his gaze over Trip's apartment. She'd left one small lamp on, creating a warm, golden glow.

''A loft,'' he said. ''Dynamite. I really like your home, Alice.'' But how did she pay the rent for this place on her current salary?

''Thank you,'' she said, her gaze lingering on the screens she'd moved from in front of the bed to the opposite side of the expanse. ''I was lucky to find it when I moved back here. It's perfect for...my needs.'' She paused. ''Would you like something to drink? Oops. I think I'm supposed to ask you if you want coffee.''

''No, I don't want any coffee.'' Brent closed the distance between them. ''I want—'' he cradled her face in his hands and dipped his head to outline her lips with the tip of his tongue ''...you.''

Shivering at the sensuous foray, Trip whispered, ''And I want you.''

Trip stepped back, causing Brent to drop his

hands from her face. She took one of his hands in hers and led him across the large room to the double bed that was streaked partially with shadows. She turned to him, her arms floating up to encircle his neck. He wrapped his arms around her and claimed her lips in a searing kiss.

Brent ended the kiss slowly, reluctantly, savoring the taste of Alice, the feel of her breasts crushed against his chest, her aroma of spring flowers and woman. He drew his hands down her arms, then kissed the fingers of both of her hands before releasing them.

Trip swept back the blankets on the bed, then lifted her chin and met Brent's smoky gaze. With hands that were not quite steady, they removed their clothes, fumbling at times, Brent swearing under his breath at the repeated motions and wasted time. Then they stood there…naked before each other, drinking in the sight of what was displayed for them, only them.

"You're exquisite, Alice." Brent's voice was raspy with passion.

"So are you," she said, hearing the thread of breathlessness in her voice.

She moved onto the bed and waited…an eternity…for Brent to retrieve a foil pack from his wallet. He stretched out next to her, propping his weight on one forearm.

"Alice," he said huskily, "we are going to go to Wonderland together."

And they did.

They kissed and caressed, explored and discovered the mysteries being revealed to them of a body so soft and feminine, and one so rugged and male, etching all they found indelibly in their minds...and hearts.

Brent drew the lush flesh of one of Trip's breasts into his mouth, laving the nipple with his tongue. She sighed in pure pleasure, closing her eyes for a moment to savor every heated sensation consuming her. He moved to the other breast to pay homage there, as her hands slid over his moist back, his muscles bunching beneath her palms. He skimmed one hand across her flat stomach, then along her slender hip and leg, his lips soon following the heated path.

"Oh, Brent, please," Trip said, her voice holding an echo of a sob. "I want...need...now...I..."

"Yes," he said, hardly recognizing the gritty sound of his own voice.

He took the necessary steps to protect her, then his mouth melted over hers once more before he entered her with a deep, powerful thrust, filling her, bringing to her all that he was.

She gripped his shoulders as he began the rhythmic tempo, slowly at first, then increasing it, faster, harder, thundering. Trip matched him beat for heart-stopping beat in perfect synchronization.

Higher they went. Heat coiled and tightened, sweeping through them in waves of ecstasy that held the promise of the moment yet to come, the place they would be flung to. Wonderland.

"Brent!"

"Alice. Oh, Alice."

There was a kaleidoscope of colors, so vivid, so rich, swirling around them, encasing them in a cocoon where no one else was allowed entry. It was theirs. They spun out of control, clinging to each other, knowing they were safe as long as they were together. They hovered there, shifting, drifting, feeling the last ripples of release whisper throughout them.

Brent collapsed against Alice, spent, sated, then gathered the last ounce of strength he possessed to move off her and roll to her side, tucking her close to him, lips resting on her damp forehead.

Trip splayed one hand on the moist, dark curls on Brent's chest, feeling his heart begin to return to a normal beat just as hers was. Their bodies cooled, and Brent reached down to pull the blankets over them.

Neither spoke.

They searched their minds for the proper words to describe the beauty of what they'd just shared, the awe of it, then gave up in defeat as they realized that the words they needed had not yet been invented.

"Will you stay?" Trip finally said. "The night? With me?"

"I'll stay. This is where I want to be, Alice."

"This is where I want you to be," she said, then closed her eyes and slept.

Brent woke to the sound of water running in the shower, and the warmth of sunlight tiptoeing across his face. He laced his fingers beneath his head on the pillow and stared up at the ceiling.

Incredible, he thought. That was just one of the words he could use to describe the lovemaking shared with Alice. But the memories themselves were far better than any adjectives he might come up with.

Heat rocketed through Brent's body, and he shifted slightly in the bed, telling himself to change the mental subject.

Okay, he thought, he wouldn't dwell on making

love with Alice, he'd think about Alice herself, the woman. Man, she was something, really fantastic. Yes, she was complicated, had an intense side to her that caused her to scurry behind her protective wall if she began to feel pressured or pushed.

She also had a rather disturbing attitude about not being capable of being in a serious relationship.

Why that bothered him, he didn't know. Heaven knew he wasn't in the market for a serious relationship. He'd been down that road once and had vowed never to retrace those steps. He should count Alice's stand as more points in her favor but...forget it. That was too heavy a subject before morning coffee.

Alice, Brent mused on. There was also a fun, whimsical part of her that surfaced when she relaxed and just enjoyed herself. Her dark eyes sparkled, and her smile and laughter were real. She had a what-you-see-is-what-you-get honesty that he cherished, that he knew was very important to him. She was a waitress in a crummy café and if anyone had a problem with that...tough. Yes, she was reluctant to talk about herself to any great degree, but that would come in time.

The bathroom door opened and Alice appeared wearing her pink uniform. Brent drank in the sight of her, and vivid, sensuous images of the previous night formed in his mind's eye.

"Good morning," he said.

"Hello," Trip said, smiling. "I'm sorry I woke you, but I have to be at work at six, so we need to get ourselves in gear."

Meaning, Brent thought, that she preferred not to leave him here in her apartment when she left. Fair enough.

"I'll take a quick shower," he said, flipping back the blankets and leaving the bed.

"Brent, I just want to say… What I mean is…last night was…thank you."

Brent gathered his clothes from the floor, then walked past Alice and dropped a quick kiss on her lips.

"Ditto," he said. "I'd kill for a cup of coffee. Do we have enough time?"

"Yes."

Heat slithered down Trip's spine as she swept her gaze over Brent's naked body as he walked toward the bathroom. When the door closed behind him, she took a quick breath, realizing she'd nearly forgotten to breathe as she'd stared at him.

"Oh, my," she said rather dreamily. *"I will never, ever, forget last night."* She paused. *"Coffee. Make coffee, Trip. Right now."*

She had just poured two mugs full of the steaming drink when Brent emerged from the bathroom, his hair damp, his face still stubbled in a dark beard.

"I don't look too presentable," he said, running his hand over his chin, "but I'm squeaky clean. Ah, coffee. I'm forever in your debt." He took a sip of the hot brew. "Hello, my name is Brent Bardow and I just woke up."

Trip laughed. "You're so crazy. I think I've laughed more since meeting you than I did in the six months before we met."

Brent sat down at a small table and Trip settled in the chair opposite him.

"I should offer you some breakfast," she said, "but I can't because I don't have any breakfast-type food in the house and I don't have time, anyway."

"This coffee will hold me until I get back to my hotel. May I see you tonight, Alice?"

"I...I have an...appointment this evening, Brent," she said, tracing the edge of the mug with a fingertip. "I'm not certain what time I'll be free."

"An appointment? At night?"

Trip met his gaze. "Yes."

"All right," he said. "Try this on for size. I'll stay put in my room at the hotel, and you come by when you're finished with your...appointment. We'll have a late dinner. Sound feasible?''

''I'd like that.''

''All the Bardows and Renaults are staying at the Excaliber. I'm in room 610.''

Trip nodded. Brent drained his mug and got to his feet. ''I'm outta here,'' he said. ''I'll see you tonight. Walk me to the door?''

At the door Brent kissed Trip so intensely that her knees began to tremble.

''Tonight,'' he said when he finally released her.

''Yes,'' she said with a little puff of air.

When the door closed behind Brent, Trip stared at it for a long moment, then started back toward the table and her unfinished coffee. Halfway across the room she stopped, her gaze pulled to the screens on the far wall.

Secrets, she thought, walking to the screens, then behind them. She was still keeping secrets from Brent, from her entire family. Well, Brent had secrets, too. He hadn't yet told her why he had dreaded returning to the States, hadn't shared what had happened to him in the past to evoke that negative emotion.

So many secrets.

Trip stared at what she had hidden with the screens.

There they were. The easel, the paints and brushes, the few small framed paintings she'd left there when she'd taken the large ones to Denny's.

There they were. Her hopes, dreams, the focus of her existence.

There they were. Her secrets.

And tonight she and the agent she'd hired upon returning to Ventura were meeting with the owner of a prestigious gallery to discuss the possibility of an exclusive showing of her work. Trip had already sold some of her pictures on the beaches and in small galleries up the coast, and that money allowed her to pay the rent on her loft. But this could be her big break.

Her work. The paintings she signed with an *A* in the lower right-hand corner. An *A* for Alice, because when she painted she was no longer the rebel Trip, the confused and angry Trip, searching for her own identity. When she painted she was free in her mind, her spirit, her very soul. She was Alice, and when she painted she embraced the very essence of who she was.

Just as she had done when she'd made love with Brent Bardow.

But the majority of the time, she thought with a sigh, walking slowly back to the waiting coffee, she was still Trip and had been for many, many years.

Trip, who didn't even know how to reach out and embrace the unconditional love of her family, let alone lower her self-made barriers enough to give her heart to a special man.

She sank onto the chair at the table, then stared across to where Brent had sat.

When she was with Brent, she mused, she was vitally alive, free of her inner ghosts and demons. When she was with Brent, her smiles were real and genuine laughter flowed easily from her lips.

When she was with Brent, she was beautiful and acutely aware of her own femininity, her woman-liness.

"Caring and sharing," Trip said aloud.

Brent was teaching her how to do that and it felt like a warm, comforting blanket she could wrap around herself and savor.

Chapter Five

Trip walked slowly along the crowded sidewalk leading to the Excaliber Hotel, attempting and failing to blank her mind.

She'd had the taxi let her out two blocks away with the hope that the added distance would enable her to settle down to earth after the exciting meeting with her agent and the owner of the art gallery.

She'd even gone home to change into jeans and a nubby, lightweight white sweater before starting out for the late dinner with Brent. But even that diversion hadn't stopped her mind from replaying every word that had been spoken at the gallery.

"Unbelievable," Trip whispered.

In a little more than two months, she was to have a private, invitation-only showing of her work at one of the most prestigious art galleries in Ventura, California.

A shiver of pure joy coursed through her and she wrapped her hands around her elbows to hug the wondrous sensation, to keep it safely within her so she could savor every precious moment of it.

After so many years of pinching pennies to buy supplies needed for her work, of spending endless hours alone concentrating on her painting, cutting herself off from her family, as well as the people she'd come to know, the solitary life she'd led had finally resulted in her being recognized as a talented artist.

"Unbelievable," Trip said again, but in the next instant she frowned as a chill swept through her.

Her heartfelt dream, her deepest desire, was coming true, she thought, and she had no one to share the glorious news with.

She just couldn't envision herself calling a meeting of the MacAllisters and saying, "Guess what? I know that I haven't acted like a member of this family for many years, but now I want you to forget all that and be sincerely thrilled for me. I've accomplished what I set out to do, which was, of course, something you knew absolutely nothing about." No, that was asking far too much.

Trip sighed, glanced at her watch, then quickened her step when she saw that it was nearly nine o'clock.

Sharing and caring, she thought. Brent placed great emphasis on that, but she couldn't tell him what had transpired this evening, either. It was all too new and she felt so fragile, as though she was hanging on to what had happened by her fingertips, afraid it would somehow disappear into oblivion and not really be true.

Trip entered the hotel and started across the expensively decorated lobby, headed toward the bank of elevators. And ran smack-dab into King Chester, Charlane and Byron Bardow, Maggie and Devon and Maggie's parents, who had just walked out of the restaurant on the main floor.

Oh, good grief, Trip thought, where was the rabbit hole to fall into when Alice needed it?

"Trip," Maggie said, smiling. "What are you doing here?" She laughed. "That was a silly question. You must be meeting Brent."

"Who refused to have dinner with us," Charlane said pleasantly, "because he said he already had plans for a late supper. The salmon was delicious, dear, and came with a dill sauce to die for. You might mention that to Brent. He enjoys salmon when it's cooked to perfection the way they do it here.''

''I'll...tell him,'' Trip said, acutely aware of the flush of embarrassment staining her cheeks. ''Salmon and dill sauce. Got it.''

''Did Bobby find you and give you a cell phone?'' Maggie said. ''My brother is coming unglued about this baby that's about to arrive. It's so cute. I've never seen him so jangled.''

''There's a lot of 'being jangled' going around these days,'' Trip said, producing a small smile. ''Yes, I have the phone and... Oh, good grief, this is mortifying. I mean, heaven knows what all of you must be thinking about me and Brent and my arriving here at this hour and...'' Her voice trailed off and she threw up her hands.

King Chester smiled. ''I do believe we're thinking that you and Brent intend to share a late dinner, my dear. There's really nothing mortifying about having salmon and dill sauce in the company of someone you enjoy being with. It's a rather common occurrence.''

''Oh,'' Trip said.

''Trip, I hope you didn't mind that Bobby gave you the cell phone,'' Maggie said. ''If you'd rather not be disturbed at heaven only knows what time when the baby decides to come into the world, I can tell him not to call you.''

"No, no, I want to be called. Really.'' There it was again, the walking on eggshells around the unpredictable and here-today-and-gone-tomorrow Trip. "I was very pleased that Bobby included me.''

"Well, if you're sure,'' Maggie said.

"Positive,'' Trip assured her.

"We've kept you from your dinner long enough,'' Charlane said. "I know my son. He's a grumpy bear when he's hungry. It was lovely seeing you again, Trip. Alice.''

"It was nice to see all of you, too.'' Trip edged around the group. "I'd better be on my way so the bear doesn't get any grumpier. Bye.''

Trip rushed to the elevators, silently thanked one that was standing open as she entered it and pushed the button for the sixth floor with more force than was necessary.

Mortifying, she mentally repeated, then stared into space. Except…now that she thought about it, *she* had been the only one who had been embarrassed when she'd encountered the Bardows, Renaults and MacAllisters.

Oh, would she ever be able to relax and just…

just *be* around her family and those connected to it? She was beginning to doubt it would ever happen.

Brent spun around from where he'd been staring out the window when he heard the rather tentative knock on the door of his suite.

"Alice," he said, aware that his heart had increased its tempo. "She's here, at long, long last."

He strode across the room and flung the door open, not taking the time to look through the safety hole.

And then he just stood there, drinking in the sight of Alice.

She was here, after a day that had seemed like a week. She was here, looking so lovely, delicate and feminine. She was here, and if he didn't take a breath in the next two seconds he was going to pass out cold on his face.

As Brent filled his lungs with much-needed air, he extended one hand to Alice. She placed her hand in his and allowed him to draw her into the room.

Brent closed the door behind Alice, then dropped her hand and moved close, causing her to bump into the door. He braced his hands on either side of her head and looked directly into her eyes, his body only inches from hers.

All the thoughts in Trip's mind disappeared into

a sensuous mist as she gazed into Brent's blue eyes. The tips of her fingers tingled with the urge to touch him, but she kept her arms at her sides.

Time lost meaning as they stood there, not moving, hardly breathing, anticipating the moment when their lips would meet. Heat began to churn low and hot within them as the tension built and their desire soared.

Then Brent slowly, very slowly, lowered his head and brushed his lips over Alice's. Once. Twice. Then returned to claim her mouth in a kiss they had waited an eternity to share.

Brent groaned deep in his chest.

A whimper of need caught in Trip's throat.

Brent broke the kiss and spoke close to Alice's lips, his body still inches away from hers.

"I missed you." His voice was rough with passion. "I thought about you all day. It's corny, it's nuts, but it's true. I am so damn glad you're here, Alice."

"This—" she drew a shuddering breath "—is where I want to be, Brent."

"Same wavelength. Perfect."

"I...I bumped into our families in the lobby," Trip said. "They know I'm here. With you. I was embarrassed, flustered, because it's so late at night, and I was obviously heading for your room and...

But they all acted like it was the most natural thing in the world, and your mother suggested you have salmon for dinner.''

Brent chuckled, and the rumbling, male sound caused a shiver to course through Trip.

"Salmon with dill sauce?" he said.

"Dill sauce," she said, nodding. "She said it was delicious and... If you don't take me in your arms right now I think my bones are going to dissolve from the heat, the incredible heat that's...oh!"

Trip's startled "Oh!" was followed by a gasp of surprise as Brent swept her up into his arms and carried her across the living room and into the bedroom beyond. He placed her on the bed, then followed her down, his mouth melting over hers. She wrapped her arms around his neck and returned the heated kiss in total abandon.

When they separated only long enough to shed their clothes, Trip felt as though she was floating above herself, watching Trip remove what she'd chosen to wear, then be magically transformed into Alice. Alice, who could simply *be*.

Their joining held an edge of urgency, of need so powerful it consumed them beyond reason. It was earthy and rough, wild and real. It was ecstasy. And heat. Burning. It was wave after wave of sensual sensations that carried them over the top and flung them into glorious oblivion as each called out the name of the other, the only one who could go with them to that private and magnificent place.

And then they stilled, and savored and stored memories in chambers of hearts that began to return to normal tempos. They drifted down from where they had been to realize that where they now were was also theirs alone to embrace.

"You," Brent said, lying close to Alice, his lips resting lightly on her forehead, "have woven a spell over me, Alice."

"That's because I'm Alice in Wonderland," she said dreamily. "I followed the white rabbit into a world of magic."

"Tell the rabbit to get his own woman. You're mine."

Trip stiffened slightly, then relaxed again, refusing to allow anything to mar the sweet bliss of the moment.

"Yes, I'm yours," she said, then paused. "For now. For the time we have while you're here and…"

"Shh," Brent interrupted. "Don't go there."

"You're right. Shh."

A lovely, serene silence fell, and sleep began to creep over their senses. Then Brent's stomach rumbled, causing a bubble of laughter to escape from Trip's lips.

"You're hungry. Your mother told me that you turn into a grumpy bear if you're not fed regularly, or something like that."

"A grumpy bear?" Brent said, smiling. "What kind of a thing is that for a mother to say about her darling kid? However, the truth of the matter is...I need food. Want some salmon with dill sauce? I'll call room service and tell them it's an emergency rush order."

"Go for it."

Less than half an hour later, Trip and Brent were dressed, seated at the table by the windows and taking their first bites of flaky salmon.

"Delicious. Your mother is a wise woman, sir."

Brent nodded. "Yep, she is. Most of the time. She gets kind of freaky on the subject of my providing her with a slew of grandchildren, though. I told her not to hold her breath and she threatened to do exactly that and her death would be all my fault."

"You don't want to have children?" Trip said, cocking her head to one side.

Brent sighed. "At one point in my life I wanted

the whole nine yards. A wife, kids, a home. But then…'' He shook his head.

''Brent, does the 'but then' have something to do with why you didn't want to make this trip with your parents? You haven't…well, shared that with me, the reason you didn't wish to return to the States. We do sharing and caring, remember?''

Brent looked at her for a long moment, then nodded.

''You're right, that's part of our program. So, yeah, okay. When I was in college I was in what I believed to be love with a woman who was getting a degree in psychiatry. I assumed, which was my first mistake, that we would marry and live on the Island of Wilshire. I later realized we hadn't discussed that in any depth, that I had just taken that fact for granted.

''Brittany, that was her name, was assuming a far different scenario. She thought that I understood she couldn't make a name for herself on a dinky little island in the middle of nowhere.''

''Oh, dear.''

''Brittany had it all figured out,'' Brent continued quietly. ''I should return home long enough to train one of my men to take over the vineyards, then come back to California and get a job with one of the big outfits here. That last scene with Brittany is not a fond memory, believe me.''

"I'm sorry, Brent. It's no wonder you didn't want to make this trip, return to a place that would bring back painful memories. But…well, I'm very glad you did.''

"So am I," he said, producing a small smile. "But what happened with Brittany made me wary of getting into any kind of serious relationship again. She had an agenda, a plan, that didn't include my wants, my needs.

"For the last few years I haven't even dated because I found myself wondering if the woman might have a secret agenda, a dream to leave the Island of Wilshire for the excitement of the world beyond it. What if I came to care for someone, only to discover…

"You know what Brittany told me, Alice? During that last ugly scene with her she said I was out of step with the times, that I'd expected her to put her career on the back burner. That I should go home to my fantasy island and find someone to wait on me hand and foot.

"She said I'd better make certain that the next woman in my life didn't have any hopes or dreams of her own. According to Brittany, I was so selfish and self-centered I couldn't deal with a woman needing more than just me to feel fulfilled.

"I've never forgotten those words she hurled at me. They leveled me like physical punches. Secret agendas. I made up my mind I'd never run the risk of going through something like that again. There you go. The great tale of woe."

"I'm…well, sad, that you had such a devastating experience. It obviously hurt you very much."

"On a much brighter note," Brent said, "my mother promised to bring me some of those dynamite Mickey Mouse ears when they all go trekking down the coast to Disneyland. Cool, huh?"

"Majorly way cool," Trip laughed. "Is that how the teenagers say that these days? Or is it awesomely majorly way cool? I'll ask Trevor and get back to you so you can refer to your new ears in the proper manner."

"Your assistance in the matter will be appreciated."

They burst into laughter, the joyous sound pushing aside the shadows of the past with the sunshine of the present, but giving no space to thoughts of the future.

They completed the meal with lively chatter that flowed easily from one topic to the next, then settled onto the sofa and began to watch an old movie on television. Trip curled up close to Brent, resting her head on his shoulder. He wrapped one arm around her, absently stroking her arm as they yelled at various people who might be the villain and cheered on the hero.

"I am *not* spending the night here," Trip said during a commercial. "I mean, good grief, with my luck I'd find your family in the elevator in the morning when I left."

Brent chuckled, then kissed her on the forehead. "They'd probably just smile and ask you to join them for breakfast. They're...wait a second, I have to say this right...they're awesomely majorly way cool people."

"Well, *I'm* not," Trip laughed. "I'd die on the spot. Nope, I'll wait until this movie is over, even though I already know the butler did it, then I'm definitely going home."

"The butler did it?" Brent said, frowning. "No, he didn't. He's not the one who tried to kill the hero. The butler is an undercover agent for the FBI. The gardener did it."

"He did not," Trip said. "He was planting marigolds when the shot was fired. The butler is really the hero's long-lost sister, posing as a man, and she wants to ice the hero before he can marry the heroine so she can inherit the family fortune."

"Have you seen this movie?"

"No." Trip laughed. "Have you?"

"Nope. Okay, now this is getting interesting. I'll bet you five bucks that the gardener did it."

"Oh, easy money. You're on, Bardow. It was the butler in drag, or whatever."

"I don't accept credit cards, MacAllister," Brent said, with a hoot of laughter. "I want my five smackeroos in cold, hard cash."

They both moaned in dismay when it turned out that the cook did it. The hero's father, long since deceased, had jilted her in her youth and she was out for revenge, deciding the son would repent for the sins of the father.

"Boo, hiss!" Brent yelled.

"Who wrote this thing?" Trip said, dissolving in a fit of laughter. "No wonder they showed it late at night. No one would waste their leisure time in the early evening to watch it. I give it a thumbs-down."

"Ditto." Brent pressed the remote to turn off the television.

"I've got to go home," Trip said, not moving. "It's already tomorrow, and I have to get up so early."

"I wish you'd stay." Brent pulled her even closer to his side. "I want to wake up next to you."

"I…"

"Hey, it's okay," he said quickly. "I understand where you're coming from. I might add, however, that Maggie is spending the night in Devon's suite and my clan knows it. That's just a little bubblegum for your mind to chew on. Data."

"Maggie and Devon are engaged to be married," Trip said, wiggling out of Brent's embrace and getting to her feet. "Big difference there."

"I won't argue the point," Brent said, rising. "This time. But it's going to be a trade-off. Don't give me grief over the fact that I'm going with you in the taxi, will see you safely home, then I'll come back here."

"But—"

"It's not open for discussion, Alice," Brent said, then paused. "The cook did it. Man, talk about having a secret agenda." He wrapped his arms around her and nestled her to his body. "You will never know how glad I am that you don't have a secret agenda, Alice. That means more to me than I could even begin to tell you."

People in general, Trip thought, would probably view her as being terribly dishonest with Brent because she hadn't told him about her art, the scheduled showing, her hopes and dreams, her secret.

But what those who would pass censure on her

actions wouldn't understand was that her *agenda,* to use Brent's word, wasn't something that would cause him to feel betrayed if he knew about it.

No, it wouldn't be like that at all, because if she and Brent were actually moving toward having a future together, her secret agenda would fit in perfectly with his lifestyle on the Island of Wilshire, where he intended to live out his days. If she told Brent about her painting, he would be so happy as he realized she could be very contented on his peaceful, beautiful island.

Trip sighed.

There was no point in telling Brent about her painting, as they were *not* viewing what they were sharing as possibly being permanent.

Besides that she hadn't yet gathered enough courage to tell Brent, or her family, about her work. Every time she envisioned herself doing that, she was consumed with icy fear, a feeling of being so exposed, so vulnerable to opinions and attitudes.... All those years of being alone still held her in an iron fist from which she was unable to break free.

Chapter Six

For Trip, the following week seemed to fly by with a speed that made her head spin at times. She should, she knew, be thoroughly exhausted from the pace she was keeping, but she was, instead, bursting with energy that kept her moving at top speed.

Life, she decided at one point, was glorious. Working at the café was something she did by rote, then her afternoons were spent painting more pictures for the gallery showing…sometimes in her loft, other times in a nearby park…and her nights were focused on Brent.

She'd gotten her car back from the repair shop

and taken the pictures she'd had stashed at Denny's to the gallery, where decisions were reached on the types of frames to be made for each. She had only three more pictures left to paint to complete the agreed-upon number for the showing of her work.

One week plus a day since the night she and Brent had eaten salmon with dill sauce in his hotel suite, they stood in line at a movie theater, waiting to inch their way forward to purchase tickets.

"Missed you today, per usual," Brent said, one arm encircling Alice's shoulders to keep her tucked close to his side. "I went to a museum this afternoon and kept seeing things I wanted to share with you, ask you what you thought, while knowing we'd be on the same wavelength. I toyed with the idea of calling and asking you to join me, but I know you need to sleep so you'll be ready to rock and roll with me in the evening."

"Mmm," Trip said.

She'd put the finishing touches on a painting this afternoon, had *not* been napping as Brent assumed she'd been, she thought.

"Is something wrong, Alice?" Brent said, bringing Trip from her troubled thoughts.

"What? Oh, no, no," she said, smiling up at him. "I'm just a little tired. I'll relax during the movie and be fine."

"Didn't you get enough sleep this afternoon?" Brent said. "We can make an early night of it if you like so you can get the rest you need."

"Feed me popcorn during the movie," she said, "and I'll be as good as new."

"You've got it, my sweet," Brent said, dropping a quick kiss on the top of her head. "I'll buy you the biggest bucket of buttered popcorn they make." He tipped his head to the side to see what was taking so long to get to the ticket window. "If we ever get into this place, that is. We're going to miss the start of the movie if they don't hustle up. Time is marching on."

Time is marching on, Trip mentally repeated. Time was the enemy. Time was going to run out and Brent would get on a plane and fly to the other side of the world, out of her life.

Yes, she'd see him again when she went to the island for the wedding, but she'd already told herself not to count on being able to spend many private hours with Brent there because of the festivities scheduled.

Dear heaven, the very thought of Brent leaving made her feel so hollow, so bleak and chilled to the core. She would reach across the bed in the darkness of night and he wouldn't be there. She'd sleep alone. She'd eat alone. She'd spend her days and nights alone.

And she would be so very, very lonely.

She felt such a sense of rightness when she was with Brent, of being complete, whole, of having found the masculine counterpart who fit so perfectly with the new awareness of her womanliness she now possessed. She cared so much for him that the thought of his leaving her made her feel cold and empty, and a breath away from bursting into tears.

Good grief, Trip thought, frowning. If someone could read her mind they might very well come to the conclusion that she was in love with Brent Bardow. But she wasn't. Dear heaven, no, of course she wasn't. Falling in love was beyond her grasp, was an emotion she wasn't capable of.

If she didn't have the courage to show Brent, or her family, her dream, her art, she was definitely not able to run the risk of allowing herself to do something so emotionally momentous as falling in love, giving her heart to someone to do with as they may. God, what a terrifying thought.

Trip gazed up at Brent, who was once again looking at the line ahead of them.

Brent was going to get on that airplane, she thought, and he was *not* going to take her heart with him. No. The deep feelings she had for him, the caring, would fade in time, dim, then be gone. She was *not* falling in love with Brent.

"Ah, here we go," Brent said. "Some guy was buying about fifteen tickets for the group with him so that took a nice chunk out of the line."

"I…oh, good heavens," Trip said, jerking in surprise. "My purse is ringing." She rummaged inside and snatched up the cell phone.

"Hello, Bobby," she said tentatively as she pressed the tiny device to her ear.

"It's happening, Trip," Bobby said. "Finally. The baby. We're at the hospital. I'm petrified. I can't breathe, Trip. I swear I…gotta go. Bye."

"Bye," Trip said, her eyes widening. "Brent, the baby is…Bobby can't breathe," Trip said, then took a sharp breath. "I can't, either. Now what?"

Brent laughed. "Now we go to the hospital and wait for the newest MacAllister to come into the world."

"You don't have to spend your evening pacing around a hospital waiting room," Trip said as they left the line of people and started down the sidewalk. "You can just drop me off if you like."

"No way. I wouldn't miss this for the world. It's not every day of the week that a person gets to be involved in a miracle."

"What a lovely thing to say," Trip said, as Brent assisted her into the car he'd rented.

Brent splayed one hand on the roof of the car and gripped the edge of the open door with the other. He bent down to look directly into Alice's eyes.

"That's what babies are, Alice," he said quietly. "Miracles. Two people made love, shared the most intimate act known to humanity and created a new life. Oh, yes, babies are miracles."

"Yes," Trip said softly. "You're right, and you're also very special for having said so."

Brent leaned far enough into the car to kiss Alice, then stepped back and closed the door. He jogged around to the driver's side and slid behind the wheel.

"Buckle up," he said, "and send messages to the stoplights to turn green as we approach them." He turned the key in the ignition. "Oh, this is great. I have no idea where the hospital is."

"I'll direct you," Trip said. "Go straight ahead for two blocks, then turn right. The hospital is where Maggie and Devon met, you know."

"Yeah, I heard the story of how they connected there. Well, that hospital is definitely a miracle-making place," Brent said as he pulled away from the curb.

A baby, Brent mused, as he maneuvered the car through the heavy traffic. A miracle. What would a baby created by Alice and him look like? Would he, or she, have blond hair like Alice's? Or black hair like his? Maybe nature would combine the two and their baby would have brown hair. Yeah, that would be nice...a blend of his parents.

Oh, man, Alice would be so exquisitely beautiful while she was pregnant with his child, and he'd be by her side every step of the way. He could envision himself placing his hand on her rounded stomach, feeling the baby move within her. What an awesome and humbling thought.

Brent blinked, then frowned.

What a ridiculous thought, he admonished himself. Where had all that nonsense come from?

He and Alice weren't going to create a baby when they made love.

They weren't going to get married and raise a family. They weren't even going to see each other again when he left Ventura, except for whatever time together they could steal when Alice came for the wedding.

And the most important "weren't" on the list was the fact that he and Alice *weren't* in love with each other in the first place, an ingredient that should definitely be in the mix.

Yes, that's what it was. A recipe. Two people met, were attracted to each other. Add sharing and caring, respect and honesty, blend well while spending as much time as possible together. Sift in smiles and laughter, and lovemaking so incredibly fantastic it defied description.

Simmer until hearts melted, then meshed into one entity strong enough to withstand the rigors of time.

Whoa, Brent thought, rolling his eyes heavenward. That was so corny it was a crime. Since when did he indulge in such romantic gooey garbage like that? Well, it wasn't really garbage, it was sort of poetic. Love, forever and ever love, was a carefully attended-to recipe that two people concentrated on making together and...

"Oh, for Pete's sake," he said, shaking his head in self-disgust.

"What's wrong?" Trip said, looking over at him.

"Huh? Oh, I got caught by this red light, that's all," Brent said.

Trip smiled. "I don't think the baby will be born before we get to the hospital." She paused. "Will it? It's overdue, I guess, so maybe it will be in a big hurry now and...forget it. I have no idea what I'm talking about. Brent, the light is green."

"Oh," he said, pressing on the gas pedal. "Alice, did you ever think about the fact that love is like a recipe? There's a whole bunch of ingredients that have to be there in the right amounts, then blended together just so. And they have to be continually tended to so that it doesn't go stale like something you baked would if you just ignored it once you... Never mind. I'm blithering like an idiot.''

''No, you're not,'' Trip said thoughtfully. ''I think you expressed that very well. Very romantically, too, I might add. Yes, love could be compared to a recipe.'' She smiled. ''I think one of the ingredients is magic.''

''Mmm,'' Brent said, nodding.

Like the magic he and Alice shared. Oh, Bardow, cut it out. He was not giving one more moment's thought to love and the stupid recipe and...because he wasn't in love, had no intention of ever falling in love again and that was that.

The fact that he felt sliced and diced whenever he thought about leaving Alice was because...was because he *cared* for her. A lot. More than a lot. Very deeply. Very, very deeply and...

''Turn right at the next corner,'' Trip said, bringing Brent from his jumbled thoughts.

''Thank you,'' he said, more than happy to direct his attention entirely to following the directions to the hospital.

"Thank you?" Trip said, laughing. "For telling you to turn right? Gosh, do I get a hug when we actually arrive in the parking lot of the hospital?"

"Sure," Brent said, chuckling.

"It's that tall building in the next block," Trip said, pointing. "See it?"

"Yep. I imagine the waiting room is going to be packed with MacAllisters."

"I don't know. I have no idea if the clan turns out in force after all these years and all the babies that have arrived. Maybe they just stay home and wait for a telephone call."

The MacAllisters definitely did not wait at home for news of the birth. The waiting room that Trip and Brent were directed to was crowded to the point that Trip's cousin, Ryan, and his father, her uncle Ted, were leaning against the wall outside the room.

"Hey, Trip, Brent," Ryan said, then shook Brent's hand. "Nice to see you here."

"This is exciting," Trip said. "How long do you think we'll have to wait before the baby is born?"

Ryan shrugged. "Don't have a clue." He laughed. "My famous top-cop dad here delivered my sister himself because she was in such a rush. Then? I was six months old before they came to Korea to adopt me. I think they were still worn out from the way Patty popped into the world four years before that.''

"Very funny," Ted Sharpe said, chuckling. "Not funny was the fact that you took one look at me and started wailing your head off.''

"You're a scary guy," Ryan said, smiling at his father. "Lean and mean.''

"Yeah, right," Ted said. "As for Bobby and Diane's baby? It's anyone's guess how long we'll all be here. Babies start running the show from the very beginning, that's for sure.''

Trip poked her head into the waiting room. She felt a little shiver of nervousness slither down her spine at the size of the group, who were all suddenly looking directly at her.

Now, she supposed, they would all make a big fuss over the fact that she was there, was joining the family for this special event. She'd become so uncomfortable that she'd want to leave in about three minutes flat and...

"Hi, sweetheart," Forrest MacAllister said, then resumed his conversation with his brother Michael.

"Hello, darling," Jillian called to her daughter. "I'm afraid there's nowhere to sit in here so you'll have to stand for now." She redirected her attention to Margaret, who was sitting on the sofa.

Trip opened her mouth, then closed it again, allowing a genuine smile to form on her lips.

No one was going cuckoo because she was here, she realized. It was as though they simply expected her to be among them because…well, because she was a MacAllister. Oh, this was nice. Very, very nice.

"You look pleased about something," Brent said, sliding one arm across Alice's shoulders.

"I'm just glad to be here," Trip said, smiling up at him.

"Alice," Robert MacAllister said, coming out of the room.

"Hello, Grandpa," she said, kissing him on the cheek. "Did you enjoy visiting Disneyland…again?"

"It brought back fond memories," he said. "Alice, remember when I announced at Christmas that I would be meeting with each of my grandchildren at a time that I chose to give them a special gift?"

"Yes, of course I remember. I thought Jessica was going to pop a seam waiting for her turn. She was always begging to open gifts early when we were growing up.

"I know that the beautiful chess pieces that Jessica put on the top of her and Daniel's wedding cake were from the gift you gave her, but she's been very secretive about the meaning behind it. In fact, I have no idea how many of your private meetings have been held.''

''That's not important,'' Robert said. ''What is of importance is that it's your turn. Are you free any time tomorrow?''

Trip's eyes widened. ''I'm next to receive my surprise? Oh, I'm getting goose bumps. Yes, tomorrow is my day off. What time would you like me to come? I don't mind getting up early and... Stop laughing, Brent.''

''I can't help it. A little eager, are you? To get this special present?''

''Well, yes. This is March, and Grandpa made his announcement at Christmas, and...just hush. Grandpa? What time?''

''Nine o'clock tomorrow morning?'' Robert said. ''In my study at the house.''

''I'll be there,'' Trip said quickly.

''Bets, bets, baby bets,'' Forrest said, coming out in the hall with a fistful of money. ''It's time to put the old tradition back into action. I was champion for a long spell, Brent, way back when, until that darn Ted Sharpe blew me out of the water. I'm figuring on regaining my title. I'm predicting a girl born within the next hour. Five bucks, folks. Let's see the green.''

"It's a boy," Brent said, pulling his wallet out of his pocket. He glanced at his watch. "In no more than twenty-two minutes from now."

"Oh, yes, easy money," Forrest said, snatching Brent's bill.

Ted, Ryan, Robert and Trip all made their predictions and produced five dollars with Trip choosing a girl in two hours and fifteen minutes. Forrest scribbled all the data on a piece of paper, then disappeared back into the room.

"I'm part of the baby bet," Trip said, smiling. "Just like—"

"One of the family," Robert said, winking at her, then returning to join Margaret on the sofa.

"Yes," Trip whispered, "just like one of the family. Just like a real MacAllister."

"Good for you," Brent said quietly, then kissed her on the temple. "You *are* a MacAllister, Alice. And you're also the most *real* woman I've ever had the pleasure of getting to know."

A warmth suffused Trip from the top of her head to the tips of her toes. She savored it, memorized how it felt, then tucked it away in the special place in her heart.

Brent won the baby bet.

With only two minutes to spare of his predicted twenty-two, Bobby came running down the hallway dressed in green scrubs.

"It's a baby!" he said. "It's a boy. Seven pounds, three ounces, fingers, toes, nose, everything. He's beautiful. He's... Diane was fantastic and..." Emotions choked off his words and he shook his head.

Hugs, handshakes, slaps on the back took place, then Forrest smacked the wad of money into Brent's outstretched hand.

"I was really starting to like you, Brent," Forrest said, "but forget it. No, you're okay. I won't be a bad sport. Man, you nailed it. How did you do that? Being the baby-bet champion will just have to be a fond memory of mine, I guess. I've lost my knack."

"You're pouting, Forrest," Jillian said, coming to where they all were standing and slipping her arm through his. "You had your days of glory. Congratulations, Brent, you're the new baby-bet champion."

"I can live with that," Brent said, stuffing the money into his wallet. "When can we see this little miracle who just earned me a bunch of bucks?"

"I'll go find out," Bobby said.

"Wait, Bobby," Trip said. "You didn't tell us what you and Diane named your son."

"I didn't?" Bobby said. "Man, I'm so frazzled, exhausted, excited and..."

"His name, Daddy." Trip laughed.

"Oh," Bobby said. "Well, Diane and I decided that we're about to add a bunch of more people to the family when Maggie marries Devon. So, in honor of those new folks we're naming the baby Joseph Devon."

"I'm honored," Devon said, from where he was standing in the doorway to the waiting room. "I really am. I can't begin to tell you what this means to me. Thank you, Bobby, and express my gratitude to Diane, too."

"Sure thing," Bobby said.

"Baby MacAllister is ready to receive his admirers," a nurse said as she approached the crowd. "I've lost count of how many times I've said that. If you'll all follow me, please?"

A few minutes later it was Trip and Brent's turn to step close to the window to peer into the bassinet that had been moved next to the glass.

"Oh," Trip said, awe very evident in her voice. "Oh, Brent, look at him. He's beautiful. Such perfection in a tiny package and...you're right he's a miracle. Hello, Joseph Devon. Welcome to the world, and welcome to the most wonderful family in the universe.'' She sniffled. ''I'm going to cry, no doubt about it.''

Brent stared at the sleeping infant, his heart thundering as he drank in the sight of the baby. The achy sensation in his throat told him that it wouldn't take much for tears to fill *his* eyes, too.

A son, he thought. A miracle. He'd long ago buried the dream of being a father, having a son or daughter, created with the woman he loved. But that dream was front-row center again and was strong and solid, refusing to budge.

Brent slid a glance at Alice and saw her dash two tears from her cheeks as she continued to smile at the baby.

A baby, Brent's mind echoed. His and Alice's child. That image was settling in right next to his heartfelt desire to be a father. Whew. He was on emotional overload.

What did they mean, these new and foreign thoughts and feelings? Did his *caring* for Alice run much deeper than he'd realized? Or was he just caught up in the moment of seeing Joseph Devon within minutes of his arrival?

Damn, he didn't know what was happening to him, but he knew that somehow, *somehow,* he had to find out what all this meant.

Brent hardly remembered the farewells exchanged in the hospital, nor the drive to Alice's apartment building. She had chattered on about the new baby, about how special it had been to be a part of the family as they all saw him for the first time. He assumed that he had commented in all the right places as Alice hadn't asked if something was wrong, or remarked that he was acting strangely.

As the couple entered the loft, Brent pulled himself from his tangled and unsettling thoughts, then realized that Alice had spoken to him and was now looking at him questioningly.

"Pardon me?"

"I asked if you wanted something to eat or drink?"

"Oh. No. No, thank you," he said, then glanced around. "It still smells like paint in here, doesn't it? The little table you mentioned that you painted is sure taking a long time to dry, I guess."

"Yes, it is," Trip said quickly. "That's because I used oil-based paint. Smelly stuff. I wasn't aware of the odor because I'm so used to it. I'll open a window."

Trip hurried across the area and fiddled with the locks on one of the windows on the far wall.

Tell him, her mind shouted. *Tell Brent about your paintings. Take him behind the screens and...no. No, not yet. Not yet. But soon. I'll share it all with*

him very soon. But, oh, God, I don't have the cour-
age...not yet.

Brent sank onto the sofa. "Joseph Devon. That was really a fantastic thing that Bobby and Diane did...naming their baby after my cousin. What an incredible honor. What a gift, a touching and important way to make it clear that we're all part of a big and unique family."

Trip opened the window, then walked slowly back and settled next to Brent on the sofa.

"Yes, it was an extremely nice thing to do," she said. "Maggie was on her third tissue the last time I looked at her, and Devon was a tad misty himself."

"Mmm," Brent said, nodding. "Just think, Alice. Tomorrow, or the next day, whenever, Bobby and Diane will take the baby home and lay him in the crib they've surely gotten ready for him. They've waited all those months and he's finally here. If it was me, I think I'd probably just stand there and watch him sleep, not want to move, not leave the nursery, or... Man, a baby. A son. They're really a family now."

"Yes," Trip said softly, "they are." She swept her gaze over the loft. "I can't envision a baby in here. It's not cozy enough."

"What about in your heart, your mind?" Brent

shifted on the sofa so he could look directly at her. "Can you envision a baby there?"

"That's not a fair question at the moment, Brent," Trip said, clutching her hands in her lap and staring at them. "We just came from seeing a newborn baby, Bobby and Diane's miracle. Something like what we experienced tonight might create emotions, yearnings, that will disappear in the dawn's light of the next day."

"*Might* is the important word, Alice. But it doesn't stop there. The emotions, the yearnings, when examined in the morning light might *not* have disappeared at all. They could very well be here to stay."

Trip frowned as she met Brent's gaze. "Why are you doing this? Pushing about emotions, yearnings, regarding a baby, being a family... What are you doing?"

Brent stared up at the ceiling for a long moment, then looked at Alice again.

"I don't know," he said, sounding suddenly weary. "I saw that baby and I...I thought I'd buried those kind of dreams deep enough that they'd never be able to surface again, but...

"Alice, whenever I think about leaving you in a couple of days I feel as though I've been punched in the gut. You mean so much to me, so damn much.

"Then when I saw Joseph Devon I...I wondered what a baby you and I would create, together, would look like..." He dragged both hands down his face. "I'm a mental mess. I don't know what's happening here, what it all means, but I really can't bear the idea of walking out of your life and never... Ah, hell, I don't know."

"I don't want you to leave, either," Trip said. "We'll see each other at the wedding, but it just won't be the same. These days...and nights...with you have been so... When you go I'll miss you..." She drew a wobbly breath that held the hint of tears. "I think I just joined your mental-mess club."

"Do you...do you think we're falling in love with each other, Alice?"

"No. No, absolutely not. We'd know it if we were." She paused. "Wouldn't we? Well, yes, darn it, of course we would, and we're not. I'm just now making progress with opening my heart to my own family. I'm not even capable of the intensity of man-and-woman love, for heaven's sake. Brent, please, let's change the subject. You *are* leaving. There's no purpose to be served by having this insane conversation."

"Isn't there? Don't you want to know what's really happening between us? Don't you?"

"No," Trip said, getting to her feet. "I'm going to have a glass of orange juice. Would you like some?"

"No, thank you." Brent rose and gripped Alice's shoulders. "I *do* want to know what this is we're sharing. So, okay, I do, you don't. It calls for a compromise, I think."

"No, I don't want to think about—"

"Compromise," Brent interrupted. "Just listen, all right? I won't bring up the subject again while I'm here in Ventura, if you promise to think about it, us, during the month we're apart before you come to the Island of Wilshire for Maggie and Devon's wedding.

"The old cliché will apply, per se. The distance, the separation, will either make our hearts grow fonder, or we'll look at each other when you arrive on the island and realize what we had here was special, but…well, temporary, and that it's over. The month apart will, hopefully, supply us with the answers we don't have."

"But—"

"Alice, please promise me you'll think about us, what might be happening here. God, what if we're soul mates, meant to be together, and we let it slip through our fingers because it's so damn terrifying, and we're still held in the grips of our past pain, our ghosts, or—''

''I...I don't know what to say, Brent,'' Trip said, unwelcome tears filling her eyes.

''Just say yes. Agree to this compromise. Say you'll think about it, us, relive the memories we've made, get in touch with your hopes, dreams, yearnings, look into the future. Please.''

No, Trip thought, feeling a rush of panic consume and chill her. She couldn't handle this. Couldn't do what Brent was asking of her. She wasn't strong enough, brave enough. She was too fragile and vulnerable.

''Please, Alice,'' Brent said, a catch in his voice. ''Say you'll do it. Say yes.''

Trip stared at Brent and saw the shimmer of tears in his beautiful blue eyes, heard the edge of desperation in his voice, felt the trembling in his hands where they were splayed on her shoulders, and knew she was defeated.

''Yes,'' she whispered.

Chapter Seven

"I'm not even going to attempt to chat with you for a while, Alice," Robert said, smiling at his granddaughter the next morning. "The meetings I've already had with my grandchildren to present them with my specially selected gift have shown me that the recipient is eager to get down to business."

Trip laughed. "Guilty. I've been awake since dawn, and it seemed as though the clock was refusing to move forward so I could come over here, Grandpa."

Robert chuckled, then got to his feet and crossed

the room to a closet on the far wall. He returned, sat down, then handed Trip a framed picture face-down that was about fourteen inches square. She took it, turned it over, then the color drained from her face as she stared at it.

"Yes," Robert said quietly, "it's one of your paintings. I've had it for about two years now, although no one has seen it but me, not even your grandmother."

"But how..." Trip started, then leaned the picture against the fireplace and met Robert's gaze. "I don't understand this. I mean..."

Robert raised one hand for silence. "Alice, I couldn't bear not knowing where you were beyond the postcard you would send. I didn't know what you were doing, if you were safe, happy. It was very difficult for all of us to cope with that."

"And I'm so sorry," Trip said. "It was so selfish and self-centered of me. I'm trying to make amends to the family for the way I behaved all those years but..." She shook her head.

"But you were pursuing your dream of becoming an accomplished artist."

"Yes, but how did you—"

"I hired a detective," Robert said. "Now, before you get angry that your privacy was invaded in that manner, please understand that I did it out of love and concern for you. Once I knew you were safe, knew what you were doing, I simply waited for you to come home, having told no one what I discovered.

"That was a hard decision to make because at times I felt your parents had the right to know that you were fine, but I kept silent. If there had been any hint that you were in trouble, needed help, I would have told Forrest and Jillian. The detective bought this picture from a group you were showing on the beach up the coast and brought it to me. You're very talented, Alice, and I'm extremely proud of you."

"Thank you," Trip said softly. "I'm...I'm going to have a private, invitation-only showing of my work at a gallery here in Ventura in a couple of months, but no one in the family knows that."

"Don't you think it's time you told those who love you what you've been doing all these years? Why the secrecy, Alice?"

"Oh, Grandpa," she said with a sigh, "it's all so complicated. Mom and Dad were aware that I liked to draw and paint when I was a child, and they always put my pictures on the refrigerator. But when I started high school, they told me that even though I obviously had artistic talent it would be best to have a marketable skill. They insisted I take computer classes, things like that.''

''And?''

''They did that out of love and the worry that I might become a starving artist or whatever if I concentrated only on my painting. I realized that years later, but at the time, in my rebellious teenage mind, I viewed it as a put-down, a rejection of my talent, as a statement that I wasn't talented *enough*.''

''Oh, my dear child,'' Robert said, frowning and shaking his head.

''I was wrong. I know that now. But that was my mind-set for so many years. So many, Grandpa, and I built such high, strong walls around myself, keeping everyone at bay. I want to really come home, be a part of this family, tell everyone about my painting, the showing I'm going to have and…but I'm terrified. Grandpa, I'm so scared. If I do that I'll be stripping myself bare, will have no more walls to hide behind.

''I'll be Alice. What if I fail, don't reach the level of success I dream about? What if I tell the family about the showing and it's a flop, none of my pictures sell, people take one look and turn around and walk out of the gallery and…''

''Alice—''

''No, Grandpa, I'm Trip.'' Tears filled her eyes.

"It's safer being Trip, don't you see? I know how to protect myself when I'm Trip."

"And Trip is lonely," Robert said.

"Oh, God," Trip said, then pressed trembling fingertips to her lips to stifle a sob, "yes."

"It *is* time to come home," Robert said gently. "It's time to be Alice, my darling." He paused. "I'm going to give you your special gift now."

Robert reached down along the side of the chair, retrieved a tissue-wrapped square object and handed it to Trip. She sniffled, accepted the gift, then placed it on her knees and removed the paper.

"Oh, it's beautiful. A pewter picture frame and it's exquisite."

"It's also empty," Robert said. "It's waiting for an eight-by-ten-inch picture to be placed in it. I want you to do a self-portrait."

"What?" Trip said.

"I want you to paint a picture of yourself to be placed in that frame," her grandfather said. "But with one stipulation. It must be a portrait of Alice. Not of Trip. Alice. It will reveal who Alice really is by the expression on your face, the emotions in your eyes. Our Alice. Understand?"

"I can't do that!" Trip said, shaking her head. "No, I…"

"Shh, shh," he said. "Take the frame with you. When the time is right, you'll paint the portrait."

"But…"

Robert got to his feet, then bent over and kissed her on the forehead. "I love you, my darling. Your entire family loves you unconditionally. Remember that."

Robert left the study and closed the door behind him. Trip wrapped her arms around the lovely pewter frame, hugging it close. She drew a shuddering breath, then gave way to her tears and wept.

The next night Trip stood in front of the mirror over the bathroom sink in the loft and practiced smiling, finally sighing and leaving the small room in defeat. She sank onto the sofa with another sigh.

She didn't feel like smiling, she thought miserably. This was the last night she was to have with Brent. The airplane flight the royal family was booked on was scheduled to leave very early tomorrow morning.

Then Brent would be gone.

Dear heaven, it was so stark, so harsh, the reality of that thought.

Trip got quickly to her feet as she felt the sting of threatening tears in her eyes. She wandered around the loft, then went behind the screens and stared at the empty pewter frame she'd hung on the wall.

A self-portrait, she thought. That's what she was supposed to paint and place in the lovely frame. But it had to be a picture of Alice, not Trip. Oh, why was her grandfather doing this to her? Didn't he understand that she just wasn't ready for this? She couldn't do it, she just couldn't, because...

A knock on the door caused Trip to jerk, then she spun around and hurried to answer the summons.

Brent, her mind hummed. He was taking her out to dinner at a fancy restaurant. She would have to reach deep within herself for the fortitude to be cheerful and pleasant, not put a damper on this special evening.

Get it together, Trip, she told herself, then opened the door.

"Hi," Brent said quietly, no hint of a smile on his face as he stepped into the room.

"Hi," Trip said, closing the door behind him. "I was going to go shopping for a new dress for tonight, but I just didn't have time. So I'm wearing the one I had on the night we met, and I'm sure that's breaking some sort of rule in the dating book for you to see me in the same dress so soon...oh, Brent, I don't want you to leave Ventura."

"Ah, Alice," he said, wrapping his arms around her, "I don't *want* to leave Ventura."

Trip encircled Brent's waist with her arms and leaned her head on his chest. They just stood there, savoring the feel and aroma of each other, holding fast, not wishing to let go.

"We're a fine pair, aren't we?" Brent said finally. "We're supposed to be going out for a night on the town, and we're acting as though we're headed to dentist appointments. For root canals."

Trip laughed, a rather wobbly, tear-filled laugh. "I know. I'm trying very hard to be bubbly, shall we say, but I'm failing miserably."

"We won't think about the fact that I'm leaving tomorrow," Brent said firmly. "As of right now it's erased from our minds. What did your grandfather give you yesterday morning for your gift?"

Trip stepped back and out of Brent's embrace and met his gaze.

"Oh, you're sneaky," she said, actually producing a genuine smile. "You just slid that in there so smoothly, hoping I'd answer without thinking first. I told you last night that it was a private, sort of secret thing that is just between me and Grandpa."

"I know, I know," he said, matching her smile, "and I respect that, I really do. But a part of me is so curious I can't stand it. Mature, huh?" He glanced at his watch. "We'd better go. I made reservations."

Trip picked up her purse and shawl from the sofa and they left the loft.

Don't think about tomorrow, Trip told herself.

Just concentrate on tonight, Brent ordered himself.

The restaurant was one of Trip's favorites and was where her parents had taken their triplet daughters to celebrate their sixteenth birthday.

"Are you a mind reader?" Trip said when they were seated at a small table. "I adore this restaurant. It's so elegant and the food is delicious."

"No, I didn't read your mind," Brent said, then cocked an eyebrow at her, "but it's an interesting idea. There are times I do believe that would come in very handy in regard to you. But the truth of the matter is, I called your mother and asked her where she thought I should take you tonight. She told me to bring you here."

Trip's eyes widened. "You went to all that bother? Well, my goodness, I feel very special."

Brent looked directly at her, his expression now serious. "You *are* special, Alice, more than I think you even realize. These two weeks with you have been... I'll be counting the days until you arrive on the island and I can see you again, hold you again.... Do you suppose I should change the subject?''

"It would be a good idea," Trip said, nodding. "Oh, here we go. There's a waiter zooming this way. We'd better decide what we want to eat."

"I'm not very hungry."

"Brent," Trip said, leaning slightly toward him, "we're going to have a lovely time this evening. That will start with us enjoying a scrumptious meal. Pick something from the menu."

"What are you going to have?"

Trip sighed. "I'm not certain I can swallow one bite." She paused and flipped open the menu as the waiter stopped at the table. "Cancel that. I'm starving. I'm going to eat every bite of—" she swept her gaze over the selections "—shrimp scampi."

The waiter took both of their orders, including the request for a bottle of Renault-Bardow wine, then hurried away. Across the room a man slid onto the bench in front of a piano, then began to play and sing along.

"Isn't that music nice?" Trip said. "They didn't have that before, but it has been years since I've been here. He has an excellent voice, and he's singing so you can hear him but it doesn't intrude on conversation."

"Mmm," Brent said, poking a fork in his salad. "They didn't make flowers out of the radishes here like they did at that other restaurant. On the night we met." He lifted his head slowly to look directly at Alice. "The night that changed my life as I've known it to be for so many years. A night I will never, ever forget."

"I'll never forget that night, either, Brent," Trip said. "Nor any of the nights, days, hours or minutes that followed. I—"

"Ladies and gentlemen," the piano player said, "please excuse the interruption, but I have had a request for a special song to be sung to a special lady." He paused. "Alice in Wonderland, this is for you."

"What?" Trip said, stiffening in her chair.

"Just listen," Brent said.

Tears misted Trip's eyes as she heard the first words of the song "Look at Us" being sung…just for her.

"*Our* song," Brent said.

"Oh, dear God," Trip said, as she dashed two tears from her cheeks. "I'm going to fall apart. Thank you, Brent, for… No, I just want to listen to…*our* song."

With the music came the magic.

All gloomy thoughts were whisked into oblivion

and replaced with a rosy mist that seemed to swirl around Alice and Brent. They weren't in a bustling restaurant, they were in a land of wonder that had been created just for them. The song ended but they still heard the lovely, romantic words and the lilting melody that floated over and through them with a gentle, warming touch.

They finished their meal but couldn't have said what they ate, nor did the Renault-Bardow wine prompt them to remark on its excellence. Nothing had meaning or importance beyond the one they gazed at, drank in the sight of, cherishing and savoring every detail, look, smile, brushing of hands that lingered.

Alice in Wonderland borrowed the magical flying carpet from Aladdin and transported them back to her loft, where clothes were whisked away by the wave of Cinderella's fairy godmother's wand. They tumbled onto the bed that the Three Bears had declared to be just right, then Alice reached for Brent and he gathered her into his embrace.

Their lovemaking was slow and so very sweet, familiar, yet new. The rosy mist took on a deeper hue as their desire consumed them.

Their joining carried them up and away to the glorious place that was meant only for them, flinging them into the land of ecstasy at the very same time.

And through it all…it was magic.

They slept, only to waken again as Snow White and Sleeping Beauty had done from the kiss of the prince. Through the hours of night they tucked beautiful memories away in private chambers of hearts filled with the essence of the other.

The light of dawn tiptoed into the room with a hush and nudged them awake to face the truths of reality.

"I have to go," Brent said, his lips resting lightly on Alice's forehead.

"I know," Trip whispered.

"Stay right where you are. I want to remember you just like this, take this memory of you with me."

"Yes, all right, but I should say goodbye to your family."

"No. They wouldn't expect you to get up this early to see us off," Brent said, then paused. "Alice, I know I said I wouldn't bring this up again, but I need to hear you say it. Say you'll think about what this might be that is happening between us. Promise me. Please."

"I promise." She splayed her hand on Brent's

chest so she could feel the steady beat of his heart beneath her palm. "I promise, Brent."

"Good. That's good. Thank you."

She sighed. "I...I believe it would be best if we didn't speak on the phone, or write letters, during this month we'll be apart. We need to focus inward, look for the answers to the questions... God, a whole month until I see you again, then when we're on your island everyone will be there, and we'll be so busy with the festivities and..."

"We'll find a way to be alone," he said. "We will. I have to go. I don't *want* to go. That settles it. I *refuse* to go."

Trip laughed softly. "You sound like a spoiled brat, Mr. Bardow."

"Oh, yeah, Ms. MacAllister?" he said, chuckling. "If I flop on the floor and kick my feet will I get to stay?"

"Tantrums are not rewarded by the tantrumee getting what he's after."

"Well, damn." Brent tightened his hold on Alice, as though he intended to never again let her go. "Ah, man, this is awful. Just terrible. The bummer of the century. Grim, really grim. And if I don't get out of here I'm going to miss that plane and be murdered by people who will forget that they love me."

He eased back so he could look directly into Alice's eyes, then groaned aloud when he saw tears shimmering in their beautiful brown depths.

"Oh, don't cry," he said. "You'll rip me to shreds. Cry later, or something. I…hell."

Brent captured Alice's lips with a searing kiss that held an edge of roughness and desperation, of emotional need so intense, it stole the very breath from their bodies.

With all the willpower he possessed, Brent broke the kiss and left the bed. He dragged on his clothes, extended a trembling hand toward Alice, then snatched it back and strode across the room and out the door, closing it behind him with a click that seemed to echo like a jarring explosion through the loft.

"Goodbye, Brent," Trip whispered, then gathered his pillow to her, closed her eyes and buried her face in it, savoring his aroma and the warmth from where his head had lain.

And then she cried because she already missed him, was already lonely, was already aching for the sight of him. She already missed his touch, his smile, the sound of his laughter and that throaty chuckle of his that never failed to cause shivers of desire to slither down her spine.

Trip cried because now she was left with only

her own thoughts and emotions that were so confusing and so very frightening.

She cried until there were no more tears left to shed, then she slept, her head nestled on Brent's pillow, which was now damp from her tears.

Chapter Eight

By the end of the following week, Trip was so tired she knew she could not continue on with the plan of working at the café from early morning to midafternoon, then painting during the remainder of the day and into the evening.

Adding to the exhausting schedule was the fact that she wasn't sleeping well. She only dozed, then woke with a start and reached for Brent, who was never there.

Memories of their wondrous time together would tumble through her mind, causing her to stare up into the darkness, missing Brent.

Each time she attempted to get in touch with herself, to think about what might be happening between them as she'd promised him she'd do, she skittered emotionally away, telling herself she didn't yet have the courage to find the answers to those questions.

Her mind often played a torturous game of tug-of-war that was also depleting.

One minute she believed that she was not capable of giving her heart to a man for all time.

Then another argument would push its way forward: since she was definitely making progress in her quest to be comfortable with her family, wasn't it also possible that she might be capable of falling truly and deeply in love?

Was she in love with Brent Bardow?

No, no, she couldn't, wouldn't, examine her inner feelings too closely. Not now. Not yet. It was too frightening. Just too terrifying.

She'd drift off into a restless slumber, only to wake and repeat the turmoil, so acutely aware through it all of how much she missed Brent, and of how very, very lonely she was.

When she fell asleep in a chair in the kitchen of the café during her break a week after Brent had left, Trip knew she had to quit the waitressing job. She was running the risk of becoming physically ill from exhaustion and would be unable to complete the required number of paintings for the gallery showing.

Trip told Poppy she was sorry she couldn't give him two weeks' notice but she wouldn't be back the next day. She mentally crossed her fingers that none of her family would drop by the café for the pie she'd recommended and discover that she no longer worked there.

That night in her loft Trip stared, as she did every night, at the empty pewter frame hanging on the wall. She shook her head and started to walk away, then stopped and looked at the frame again over her shoulder.

She could, she supposed, sketch a basic outline of her head, hair, the shape of her face. That might ease her guilty conscience as far as not even attempting to paint the portrait as her grandfather had instructed her to do. She loved her grandpa so much, hated the idea that she might fall short in his eyes by not fulfilling his request.

Yes, this was a good idea, Trip thought, settling on the stool in front of the easel.

She tacked in place a sheet of special paper she used when she decided to draw a particular picture first, instead of reaching for a brush right from the beginning as she did most often. She definitely did *not* have the courage to begin the self-portrait without the safety net of sketching it first.

An hour later Trip had completed the basics of the portrait, not even considering adding her features. She nodded in approval.

She could, she decided, do this much in oils now, too, and would begin tomorrow night. The rest of this evening had to be spent on a seascape she was doing for the showing. Next would be the craggy, weather-beaten face of an old fisherman she'd seen in a small town up the coast and whose image was vividly alive in her mind.

And so was Brent.

Trip removed the paper from the easel, then put the canvas she was working on in place. She stared at the picture but saw only Brent in her mental vision.

What was he doing now, right now? she wondered. Was he thinking about her? Yes. Yes, he was, she just somehow knew that at that exact moment, Brent Bardow's mind and, well, maybe even his heart, was focused on her. She could feel his presence as though he was right there next to her about to reach out and draw her into his arms, then lower his head and kiss her and...

Trip blinked, then drew a shuddering breath as heat suffused her, swirling low and hot within her and causing her breasts to ache for the soothing touch of Brent's strong but gentle hands.

"I miss you, Brent," she whispered.

At that same moment, the first streaks of a gold and crimson sunrise were inching from the horizon as Brent stood on a hill above the vast vineyards of Wilshire, his hands shoved into the back pockets of a faded pair of jeans.

"I miss you, Alice," he said aloud, staring at the sky as the glorious colors grew bigger, pushing away the darkness of night.

He jerked and snapped his head to the side, having felt for a second that Alice had actually tapped him on the shoulder to get his attention, to let him know that she was there next to him, waiting for him to take her into his arms and kiss her, hold and touch her.

A chill swept through him as he faced the stark reality of his aloneness, knew that Alice was far, far away, the distance perhaps measured not just in miles, but in Alice's emotions as well.

What was she thinking? Brent wondered. About them. About what was transpiring between them, what it all meant. Had she already reached the conclusion that what they had shared had been special, but was now over? Was she giving way to her ghosts and hiding behind the walls she'd built around herself, her heart? No, please, no.

Brent turned and swept his gaze over the lush land behind him.

Here, he thought, nodding. This was the place. This was where he wanted to build the house that would become a home filled with love and laughter, children, the little miracles created with the woman who had stolen his heart for all time.

For him the questions were answered.

He was deeply and irrevocably in love.

With Alice.

And he was filled with the greatest joy and the greatest fear he had ever known.

Because he didn't know if Alice MacAllister was in love with *him*.

Brent sighed and dragged both hands down his face.

Man, he was tired, he thought. The day had just begun and he was weary to the bone starting out. He'd hardly slept since he'd returned to the island, had spent his nights tossing and turning, and missing Alice. But here, in the place where he belonged, his world, his little slice of heaven, he'd discovered the truth and the incredible depth of his love for his Alice.

God, how he missed her. Ached for her. Wanted,

needed, to feel her nestled close to his body, hear her laughter, see her smile, inhale her aroma of fresh air and flowers.

Alice. His soul mate. The woman he'd come to believe he'd never find but *had* found, and had envisioned as his wife, the mother of his children, his partner in life until death parted them.

Three weeks, he thought as he began to walk down the rise. There were three hellish weeks left before he would see Alice again, before he could declare his love to her, then hope and pray that she loved him in kind. Three agonizing weeks.

"I'm not going to survive this," Brent muttered. "Alice will arrive on the island and find a blithering idiot. Me. I will have slipped over the edge of my sanity and…"

Damn it, he fumed. Why had he agreed that it would be best for Alice and him to not have any contact during the month they would be apart so they could think clearly and… Wait a minute.

He *hadn't* agreed to that condition of no contact between him and Alice. He had memorized every detail of his last night with Alice, remembered when she'd made that statement and also recalled that he hadn't commented on it, one way or another. He couldn't be held to something that he hadn't really agreed to.

Brent stopped so suddenly that he staggered, then smacked into a tree, bumping his head and swearing loudly as he rubbed the throbbing spot.

"Cripes, I'm losing it," Brent said, shaking his head. "My poor parents. Their only kid is not the brightest crayon in the box. I am, actually, edging very close to being certifiably insane."

"You won't get any argument from me about that statement," a man said, coming through the trees and startling Brent. "You're to be commended for figuring that out all by yourself, Brent. It will save a hassle when they come to carry you away."

"Not cute, Peter," Brent said to the foreman of the vineyards.

Peter chuckled and the two men fell in step and walked in silence for several minutes.

"Tell me something, Peter," Brent finally said. "How long have you been married?"

"Thirty-seven years this summer," Peter said, smiling, "and I'm alive to say that because I never once forgot Lynn's birthday, or our anniversary. Oh, and Valentine's Day. That's a biggie for women."

"But there's a helluva lot more to it than just presents on the appropriate day," Brent said. "Love is...love is like a recipe and all the ingredients have to be there in the proper measure with both people working together to produce the desired result.''

''Well,'' Peter said, running one hand over his chin, ''that's a tad flowery for my way of thinking, but I get your drift. All I know is that I love Lynn even more today than when I married her. She's my wife. She's my life. Pure and simple.''

''Ah, that's really nice,'' Brent said, punching Peter on the arm. ''She's my wife. She's my life. Man, that is something.''

''Yeah,'' Peter said, eyeing Brent warily. ''You sure are in a weird mood this morning, boss. If I didn't know better I'd think that you're… Well, for heaven's sake, that's it, isn't it? You're in love. I'll be damned. Who is she? The island gossip mill says you haven't even dated anyone on Wilshire in a couple of years.''

Peter paused and his eyes widened. ''But you just got back from Ventura, California. But, hell's fire, even an old guy like me knows that long-distance relationships are not the way to work together on your recipe for love.''

''I realize that, Peter. But she doesn't have a se-cret agenda that would make her insist on living in the States. She could be happy here, I just know it. What I *don't* know is if she's in love with *me*.''

Peter shrugged. ''So, ask her.''

"I can't. Not yet. It's rather complicated but I sure as hell can tell her how I feel about *her*. And I'm going to."

"That's a start."

"Yeah, well," Brent said wearily, "I have a knot of cold terror in my gut that it might be the finish because it won't be what she wants to hear." He narrowed his eyes. "I think I'll wait a few hours before I telephone her because with the time difference from here to there she'll be asleep when the call comes. If she's sort of foggy I have a better chance of getting to say what's on my mind, in my heart, without her cutting me off. You know what I mean?"

"That's sort of sneaky."

"Desperate men take desperate measures, Peter," Brent said. "And I'm definitely desperate."

Trip was sleeping so close to the edge of the side of the bed where Brent had slept that when the telephone rang she jerked awake, then with a shriek fell off the bed and landed squarely on her bottom with a painful thump.

The telephone shrilled again.

"Ow. Darn it, that hurt," Trip said, crawling back onto the bed, then across it to snatch up the receiver of the telephone on the nightstand next to her side of the bed. "What!"

"Uh-oh," a deep voice said. "This isn't starting out so good."

Trip snapped on the small lamp on the nightstand, then flopped onto her back, deciding that the caller obviously had the wrong number but sounded so much like Brent that her heart had done a funny little two-step. This was not fair, not fair at all.

"You have the wrong number," she said, with a sad little sigh.

"I do? No, I don't. That's you. Ah, man, it's so great to hear your voice, Alice."

Trip sat bolt upright on the bed, her eyes widening. "Brent?"

"Yes, it's me. But listen a minute, okay?" he said quickly. "I want to be very clear on this issue. *You* stated we shouldn't have any contact during this month we're apart, but *I* didn't agree to that. Believe me, Alice, I remember our last night together and I *did not* comment one way or the other when you presented that plan."

Trip narrowed her eyes and mentally relived that last night with Brent.

"You're right," she said slowly. "You didn't say anything about—"

"Alice," Brent interrupted, "why are you so

wide awake? I mean, it's the middle of the night there and I thought you'd be rather…zoned if I called now.''

Trip glanced over at the edge of the bed she'd tumbled off.

"It was a rather…startling awakening,'' she said. ''Brent, you're making it sound as though you planned this call to come when I'd be at a…I don't know…disadvantage, so to speak, spacey, or something.''

''Yes, that was the idea, which obviously failed miserably.'' Brent paused. ''Alice, I miss you so much. I can't sleep, have to force myself to eat…I'm a complete wreck.''

''Me, too.''

''You are? You're a wreck? Oh, man, that's great to hear.''

''Thanks a bunch,'' she said, sinking back onto the pillow.

''Alice, I know we're supposed to be using this month to attempt to determine what's happening between us. The thing is, I've already figured it out…for me, at least. I have the answers to the questions. I know exactly how I feel about us.''

''You do?'' Trip said, a shiver of cold fear coursing through her.

Oh, dear heaven, she thought frantically, had

Brent purposely telephoned when he thought she'd be half asleep so he could tell her that what they'd shared had been no big deal? Would he then hang up before she could react and cause a messy, emotional scene?

"Yes, I do," Brent said. "I know without the slightest doubt in my mind."

"Well...that's...interesting," she said, her hold on the receiver tightening. "I guess."

"Okay, here I go. I'm going to tell you now, so just hear me out. Okay?"

Trip nodded, then shook her head slightly in self-disgust as she remembered that Brent couldn't see her.

"Yes," she said, "I'm listening."

"Alice MacAllister," he said, then cleared his throat, "I, Brent Bardow, am totally, completely, irrevocably, forever and ever in love with you."

Trip opened her mouth, closed it, blinked, then tried again. "I beg your pardon?"

"I love you, Alice in Wonderland," Brent said quietly. "I love you with all that I am as a man. I want to marry you, create little miracle babies with you, live out my days with you, here on the Island of Wilshire."

"But—"

"No, no, don't say anything," Brent said.

"You're still to have your month to get in touch with yourself, find *your* answers. It's just that you didn't have all the proper data while you were doing that, so I called to tell you that I love you beyond measure.

"I thought if you were sleepy I could just declare my love for you and hang up. But you're wide awake so I'm begging you to please not make a hasty decision or comment, or whatever, about what I just told you."

"But—"

"I'll be waiting here for you, Alice. I'll be waiting for you and for your reply to my proposal of marriage. I'll be waiting for you on the Island of Wilshire, the place, I hope, pray, you'll view as your future home...with me. I love you so much. Good night, my darling Alice."

"But..." Trip said, sitting up in bed again. "Brent?" The dial tone buzzed in her ear. "Brent?" She shook the receiver. He'd hung up?

Sudden unexpected tears filled Trip's eyes and she didn't know if they stemmed from wondrous joy or stark terror. She placed the receiver down then had to give a firm directive to her fingers to release her tight grip. She snapped off the lamp, then slid down in the bed, pulling the sheet up and holding it tightly beneath her chin with both hands.

"Brent Bardow is in love with me," she whispered.

Then Alice MacAllister, having no idea that her emotions echoed those of the man halfway around the world, those of Brent Bardow, was filled with the greatest joy and the greatest fear she had ever known.

Chapter Nine

During the next two weeks, Trip worked diligently on her paintings for the showing. She took time off to go clothes shopping with her mother and sisters and had a lovely time with her family, a fact that suffused her with warmth and happiness. Her smiles had been genuine, her laughter real, during the day they spent together going from store to store, stopping only long enough for a quick lunch.

When Jillian had taken Trip aside that day and told her that her parents would like to purchase the expensive airplane ticket for the trip to Wilshire, Trip had been deeply touched. She thanked her mother but said she had enough money in savings to pay for the fare, plus all the clothes she was buying.

"You do?" Jillian said, frowning. "But how... never mind. It's none of my business. I'll simply take credit for having done a fine job of teaching you how to handle your money while you were growing up."

Trip had smiled and nodded, but could not ignore the icy wave of guilt that swept through her. Her savings came from the sale of her pictures.

Soon, Trip had told herself. She'd gather her courage and tell her family everything...soon.

With sheer force of will, Trip did not allow herself to dwell on Brent, on his declaration of love for her, until she was alone at night during the designated time she set aside to work on the self-portrait her grandfather had requested that she paint.

It was then that she wrapped Brent's love around her like a big fuzzy blanket with a warmth that crept within her to gently caress her heart, her mind, her very soul.

She painted by rote, focusing instead on the image of Brent in her mental vision, seeing his smile, the desire in his eyes, his thick black hair that she had sifted her fingers through.

She selected memories from the treasure chest in

her heart of time spent with Brent, and she relived the ecstasy of being with him, walking, talking, smiling, laughing and making sweet wondrous love in the darkness of night.

No doubts or fears were allowed entry into the misty, sensual cocoon that swirled around her as she painted her self-portrait.

She simply savored the nearly unbelievable knowledge that she was loved by the most magnificent man she had ever known. She kept the questions regarding her own feelings at bay, not yet having the courage to examine them, seek the answers as she'd promised Brent she would do.

Three days before the MacAllister family was scheduled to leave, Trip delivered the last of the requested paintings to the gallery and basked in the owner's praise and enthusiasm for her work.

The invitations for the showing were at the printer's, the gallery owner told Trip, and a contract had been signed with a catering service that would serve champagne and canapés on the night of the showing.

The press releases had been written and delivered to the Ventura newspapers. They included the specific date on which her work would be available to the public, the day after the private showing.

Trip's agent, Delores Dano, who was overseeing

all the details, even came to Trip's loft that night to help her select what the artist of the moment would wear to the big event.

"This is silly," Trip said, as the woman examined Trip's wardrobe in the closet.

"This is image," Delores said. "Ah, here we go. This is it." She held the hanger at arm's length and nodded in approval. "Floor-length, simple but hinting at sexy with this clingy material, sophisticated, but the rose color will make you approachable, shall we say, not standoffish like basic black can be. Perfect. Trust me. I've done extensive studies on this."

"Whatever," Trip said with a shrug. "I still think it's silly. People aren't buying me, they're, hopefully, purchasing my paintings."

"Wear the dress."

"I'll wear the dress."

After Delores left the loft, Trip decided to have some dinner before putting the finishing touches on the self-portrait. She started toward the kitchen area, hesitated, then stopped.

It would be better, she decided, to look at the painting objectively, with no thoughts of Brent cluttering her mind, see what she still needed to do to it, then mull over her discoveries as she ate.

"Good plan," she said, walking to the screens she hadn't bothered to replace by the bed.

She moved around the screens, then came to such an abrupt halt that she stumbled slightly, her gaze riveted on the eight-by-ten-inch canvas on the easel a few feet in front of her.

"Dear heaven," she whispered, the rapid beating of her heart echoing in her ears.

Trip moved forward slowly, aware that her legs were trembling and she was having to tell herself to breathe, to inhale, then exhale, producing choppy little puffs of air. She pressed shaking fingertips to her lips as she stopped in front of the easel, staring at the image of herself.

She had put on canvas who she was when she was with Brent Bardow.

And it was there, shining in her eyes, in the soft smile on her lips, in the glow of her slightly flushed cheeks.

It was there.

Her love for Brent was as clear and real, honest and deep, as if she were speaking the words, declaring her feelings for him.

She was in love with Brent Bardow.

And she was Alice.

She clasped her hands beneath her chin and closed her eyes, causing tears to spill onto her face.

Free, she thought incredulously. She was finally free of the past.

And she had fallen in love. Totally, completely, irrevocably, forever and ever in love with Brent, just as he loved her.

She was Alice in a wonderland so glorious it defied description.

"I love you, Brent," she whispered as fresh tears fell. "I love you so very, very much. I'm Alice. *Your* Alice. Forever. Wait for me, Brent, there on your island. I'm coming home...to you."

The next morning Alice entered Robert's study and smiled at her grandfather, who was sitting in one of the leather chairs. She sat in the other, brushed back the tissue on the pewter frame, then handed Robert the picture. He held it carefully in both hands and stared at it intently.

"My darling Alice," Robert said, his voice choked with emotion as he met her gaze, "this is a portrait of a woman who is deeply in love and who is secure in the knowledge that she is loved in kind, is complete, has found her soul mate, her partner in life."

"Yes," Alice said, smiling as tears echoed in her voice. "I know. I do love Brent, Grandpa, and he loves me. He telephoned me from the island and told me that he loves me, then he asked me to marry him, but not to give him my answer to his proposal until I arrived on the Island of Wilshire.

"It wasn't until I painted the self-portrait that I knew how I felt about him. You are so wise, Grandpa. If it hadn't been for you requesting that I paint that picture, I might have remained too frightened to truly examine my feelings for Brent. The walls I erected around myself are gone. I can't begin to thank you for knowing me better than I knew myself, for...I'm Alice, Grandpa. I'm Alice."

The roar of the engines of the medium-size commuter plane the MacAllisters had transferred to for their final leg of the journey to the Island of Wilshire made conversation nearly impossible, a fact that suited Alice just fine.

Alice slid a glance at her mother, who was sitting next to her, then closed her eyes again.

She was so blessed to have her parents, as well as the entire MacAllister clan, Alice thought. She'd treated them all so shabbily for so many years, yet when she'd called a family meeting in her loft last night and expressed her heartfelt apology, they accepted it immediately, telling her how happy they were that she back among them.

With a voice that had been slightly shaky from nerves she'd then revealed her secret to them, including the news of the private showing. She had several paintings still in the loft that weren't going to be in the showing, and when they had looked at her work, the air had buzzed with excitement and awe.

"As you can see," she had told her family, "I sign my work with a flowing *A* in the bottom right-hand corner. That's…that's who I am…Alice. Alice MacAllister." Her voice had quivered with threatening tears. "I'm not Trip anymore. I don't need, nor want, to be Trip. I'm…I'm Alice."

That announcement, Alice mused, had produced hugs and tears and created a marvelous memory she would never forget. Then the family had helped her select a painting as a wedding present for Maggie and Devon. Everyone agreed that it would be fun not to breathe a word about her work until the bride and groom had unwrapped the gift, making it even more of a surprise. It had been such a very special, sharing evening…

"Ladies and gentlemen," the pilot said over the microphone, "please fasten your seat belts. We are about to make our approach to the Island of Wilshire."

Brent, Alice thought, lifting her head and looking out the small window. He was down there, waiting for her. Her. The woman he loved and wished to marry. Brent.

Jillian leaned past Alice to peer out of the window. "Oh, my," she said, "look at all that lush greenery. The island is bigger than I thought it was. Isn't it beautiful, Tr— Alice?" Jillian laughed. "It will take a while to remember to call you Alice, sweetheart, but believe me it's music to my ears. Oh, there, that section must be the vineyards where Brent produces that marvelous Renault-Bardow wine."

Alice nodded and Jillian settled back in her seat.

"My, my," her mother continued, "won't it be lovely to see the Renaults and Bardows again?"

Alice laughed. "Yes, Mother, I'm definitely eager to see Brent. That *was* what you were asking, isn't it?"

"Guilty," Jillian said, then kissed Alice on the cheek.

"I didn't fool you for a minute, did I? You realize, of course, that your family is very curious as to just what is going on between you and Brent Bardow. That's not being nosy. It's because we care about you, love you."

"Oh, okay." Alice smiled. "Not even a little bit nosy?"

"Well…" Jillian said, then shrugged, her eyes dancing with merriment.

"When the time is right, Mother," Alice said, suddenly serious. "I'll tell you what you want to know. But I have to talk to Brent first. Please be patient."

"I will. But don't be surprised if your father pesters you for answers. He's a loving, doting daddy, and worries himself silly about all three of his daughters, forgetting at times that you're adult women. *You're* going to have to be patient with *him.*"

"That's fine," Alice said, then looked out the window again.

Brent, her mind hummed. She could see the runway now as they made their descent to the island. She was getting closer…and closer…to Brent.

Brent stood beneath the white canopy with the other members of the royal family, as well as Maggie and her parents. Off to the right was an honor guard with two men in dress uniform with gleaming sabers and two women, one holding the flag of Wilshire, the other the flag of the United States of America in honor of the bride-to-be and her family.

Brent was dressed in gray slacks, a white shirt, gray tie and a dark blue blazer with the crest of the royal family on the pocket. A cool, late-afternoon breeze ruffled his hair, but a trickle of sweat slithered down his back. A yawn threatened and Brent faked a cough to hide it, aware that his sleepless, pacing-the-floor night was catching up with him.

"There's the plane," King Chester said. "Right on time, too."

Not exactly, Brent thought. It had taken an agonizing month for that airplane to appear through the clouds and approach the runway. Right on time? No, it had taken *too* much time. And before *this* day ended, his entire future happiness, or lack of the same, would be determined by what Alice told him.

He was a wreck. Last night he'd fantasized like an adolescent about the arrival of Alice on the island. He would step past the rest of the family, breaking all the rules of protocol, open his arms to her, and she would run across the tarmac and fling herself into his embrace. Then, not caring that there were *beaucoup* witnesses watching, he would lower his head and claim her lips in a kiss that would be...

"A perfect landing," King Chester said, jerking Brent back to the moment at hand.

Get it together, Bardow, Brent told himself firmly. *Now.*

The airplane turned at the end of the runway, then taxied back to the designated place indicated by the ground crew. A man pushed a staircase toward the plane, while another unrolled a red carpet that spread like a brilliant river from the canopy to the base of the stairs. The engines of the plane quieted, the door was opened, and Brent drew a deep, steadying breath.

As the head of the MacAllister family, Robert was first to appear in the open doorway and begin his way down the stairs, followed by Margaret. The oldest son, Michael, and his wife Jenny had been there for a month already, so the next in line was Ryan and his wife Deede, then…

Come on, come on, Brent thought, clenching his teeth. Damn, they were a big family. Let's go, let's go. Hurry up, people. He wanted, he needed, to see…

Alice.

Brent stiffened, every muscle in his body tensing as Alice appeared in the doorway then started down the stairs. She was wearing a pretty flowered dress, and the breeze was swirling it around her legs and… Oh, thank God, Alice was here. She was on the tarmac now, seemed to be looking directly at him…

Before he realized he was moving, Brent stepped from behind Devon and started forward.

"Brent," his father said, "what are you doing? This is an official royal welcome that dictates that we stand here and—"

"I don't think he gives a rip, darling," Charlane Bardow said, laughing in delight. "Protocol just flew out the window."

King Chester chuckled. "Somehow I'm not surprised. Don't worry about it, Byron. There are times when royal rules need to be broken."

"Oh, look at that," Maggie said. "Brent has stopped, opened his arms, Trip is running toward him… This is so romantic I'm going to cry. Wow! She flung herself into his arms and nearly knocked him over and now… My stars, he's kissing her."

"That's putting it mildly." Devon laughed. "I'd hate to think what we'd be witnessing if they'd been separated for *two* months, instead of one. That is one toe-curling kiss there, folks. Dad, it's time to step forward and greet the MacAllisters."

"Oh." King Chester tore his gaze from Alice and Brent. "Yes. Yes, of course. Welcome to the Island of Wilshire, Robert," he said, extending his hand. "We extend a warm and heartfelt greeting to your entire family."

"One of said family," Robert said, smiling as he

shook the king's hand, "is in the midst of her own private welcome. Well, it's not exactly private, but… We're delighted to be here."

Brent ended the searing kiss slowly and reluctantly, but didn't release his hold on Alice.

"I can't believe I did that," he said, close to her lips. "It was exactly the way I fantasized last night when I couldn't sleep. I am no doubt in deep, deep trouble with royalty at the moment, but I really don't give a damn. Ah, Alice, I am so glad to see you, missed you so much, thought you would never get here because the days, nights, hours, seconds, dragged by and…I'm blithering like an idiot. I love you, Alice MacAllister. Ah, man, I love you so much."

"Oh, Brent," Alice said, meeting his gaze with eyes brimming with tears, "I…I love you, too."

"Wh-what?" he said as his heart skipped a beat. "Would you say that again, please?"

"Brent Bardow," Alice said, framing his face with her hands, "I've found my answers. I found myself. I'm Alice. Your Alice in Wonderland, and I love you beyond measure. I truly do."

"Oh, thank God." Brent's voice was husky with emotion. He closed his eyes and tightened his hold on Alice, burying his face in her silky hair.

"Brent, darling," his mother called. "We're leaving now. It's time to give our guests a tour of the castle, dear."

Brent raised his head and sighed. "The madness begins. Hey, if you've seen one castle you've seen 'em all. Let's go to my cottage and—"

"Brent." Alice laughed, "I've never been inside a castle."

"You haven't?" he said, raising his eyebrows. "My goodness, what a sheltered life you've led. Okay. One tour of one castle coming up. *Then* I'm going to sneak you off to my cottage and... No, I'd better not start thinking about what I plan to do to you...with you...or I'll embarrass myself. Come along, Alice. Wilshire awaits your approval."

The royal home was magnificent and looked like a castle from a book of fairy tales. With one of her hands held by Brent, as though he was afraid she'd disappear into thin air if he let go of her, Alice drank in all that she saw, making no attempt to hide her awe as they moved from one beautifully furnished room to another.

She mentally cataloged an endless list of things she'd like to paint, which caused her to frown slightly as the tour continued.

As soon as she and Brent were alone, Alice

thought, she would tell him about her lifelong secret dream. She'd share the fantastic news of the private showing of her work, admitting that she was a nervous wreck about the event, afraid that none of the pictures would be purchased.

Brent would be surprised by her news, she knew, because he believed that she did nothing more than wait tables at a dinky little café in Ventura. But he would instantly realize that she could, and would, be very content on the Island of Wilshire, painting her little heart out after they were married.

Married, her mind hummed. Oh, yes, she fully intended to accept Brent's proposal, an issue they hadn't had time to address.

Alice glanced up at Brent, who was staring into space, probably, she decided, attempting not to appear too bored as King Chester explained who was who in the large portraits of past kings of Wilshire that hung on the wall in an enormous ballroom they were presently in.

The group returned to the entryway and King Chester spread out his arms.

"And there you have it," he said, smiling. "Our humble home. By now your luggage has been taken to your rooms that I pointed out to you during the tour and everything unpacked and put away. There are fresh fruit and sweet rolls there for a snack, as well. Dinner will be served at seven in the smaller dining room.

"I suggest you nap a bit. Having made the journey you just completed, I'm very aware of how exhausting jet lag can be. After dinner we'll have a festive time watching the bride and groom open some of their wedding gifts."

The king chuckled. "Do note that I said 'some' of the gifts, perhaps only those from the immediate family. Since presents have arrived from across the globe we'd be up all night if Maggie and Devon unwrapped everything they've received.

"Again," King Chester continued, "let me say welcome to the Island of Wilshire and to our home. I hope all of you are as pleased about the forthcoming wedding as I am. I've waited a long time for this, and I truly believe that my beloved wife is smiling down from the heavens on Maggie and Devon and whispering her blessings. Until seven o'clock, then."

As the king, Charlane and Byron, plus Maggie, Devon and Maggie's parents, turned and walked down the long corridor leading away from the entryway, excited chatter broke out.

Brent took one step backward, then another, tugging on Alice's hand as he moved.

"What...?" she said, looking up at him questioningly as she was drawn in the opposite direction from her family.

"Shh," he whispered. "I feel about sixteen years old but, hey, whatever works."

Alice clamped her free hand over her mouth to stifle a giggle that was a mixture of childish, mischievous fun and pure womanly happiness.

When they reached the tall, wooden, double-front doors, Jillian stopped on the stairs and looked at them.

"Remember to return to your room here in the castle in time to dress for dinner, sweetheart," she said pleasantly, then continued on her way.

Alice and Brent burst into laughter, then dashed out the doors.

Brent's cottage was about a half mile from the castle and was nestled among tall trees, prompting Alice to declare it to be the home of the Seven Dwarfs.

"Nope," Brent said. "That would make you Snow White and you're not, because you're Alice in Wonderland."

"True."

Brent had decorated his little house simply but had managed to create a cozy aura. There was one main room that included a flagstone hearth around the fireplace, a small kitchen with a dining alcove, a braided oval rug on the hardwood floor and a marshmallow-soft caramel-colored leather sofa that faced the fireplace. The sofa was flanked by a pair of brown-toned tweed easy chairs.

The walls were white and boasted only one painting, which was of the lush vineyards on the island. A bedroom and bathroom were off a short hallway to the right.

"Oh, I love it," Alice said, her eyes sparkling as she swept her gaze over the area.

"And I love *you*," Brent said, wrapping his arms around her and pulling her close to him. "And you love *me*. Ah, Alice, this is the greatest day of my life. The only thing that could make it even more perfect is if you'll say that you'll marry me. Will you? Marry me? Please?"

Alice encircled Brent's neck with her arms and looked directly into his sapphire-blue eyes.

"Yes," she said, smiling. "I, Alice MacAllister, will be honored to marry you, Brent Bardow. Yes."

"Thank you. Oh, thank you, Alice," he murmured, then captured her lips to seal the commitment to forever they had just made to each other.

Desire exploded within them, and when Brent broke the kiss he swept Alice up into his arms and carried her into the bedroom, setting her on her feet next to the double bed.

"Brent," she said, when she could catch her breath, "we mustn't do anything to take the spotlight off of Maggie and Devon. It wouldn't be fair to them. Let's not announce our engagement until after their wedding. Okay?"

"I want to yell it from the rooftops right now for everyone to hear," he said, "but I see your point. This is Maggie and Devon's time to shine, or whatever. But after we throw politically correct birdseed at them, instead of rice, and they leave on their honeymoon, we'll make our own announcement. Agreed?"

"Agreed." Alice nodded, then paused. "I would really like to share beautiful lovemaking with you now, Mr. Bardow. Agreed?"

"Oh, lady," he said, chuckling, "I am in complete agreement with that one."

"Alice," Brent said, then kissed her lips, nose, chin and forehead. "Wake up. We fell asleep after we... Alice? Come on, my love, open your gorgeous eyes. We're going to be late for dinner if we don't get moving, and I've broken enough royal rules for one day."

Alice blinked, opened her eyes, yawned, then smiled at Brent.

"Hello," she said. "I love you."

"Hello, yourself, woman that I love," he said, then glanced at his watch. "Oh, man, we're cutting this so close. Up, up, and away we go."

They actually ran back to the castle, holding hands like children who had been turned loose to play. At the front doors to the majestic structure, Brent dropped a quick kiss on Alice's lips.

"See you at dinner," he said. "I love you. Bye." He turned and sprinted off in the direction they'd come from.

"Ta-ta," Alice said dreamily, waggling the fingers of one hand in the air.

When she entered her room, she gave it a quick and appreciative perusal, then started toward the bathroom to take a shower. It wasn't until she was standing under the warm spray of water that she realized she still hadn't told Brent about her painting. They had been concentrating on lovemaking so incredibly fantastic it was beyond description, then had fallen asleep and...

Well, it didn't matter, she thought as she shampooed her hair. In fact, this would be more fun. Brent would be as surprised as Maggie and Devon about her work when the bride and groom unwrapped their present.

Then the light would dawn and he'd realize that their...what had he called it?...yes, their recipe for love was even more perfect than he'd believed it to be, because her desire to paint made her contentment as his wife there on the island a given, was guaranteed.

Alice turned off the water and stepped out of the shower. She swiped her hand across the steamy mirror to gaze at her reflection, a soft smile forming on her lips.

There it is, she thought, for all to see, just as it was in the self-portrait she'd painted. Love. Love that was returned in kind by the most magnificent man in the world.

Brent.

Chapter Ten

Dinner was a noisy, festive event with everyone sitting around a long, gleaming mahogany table in an enormous room that King Chester had referred to as "the small dining room." Roast pheasant was served with tiny new potatoes, broccoli with hollandaise sauce and a crisp, crunchy salad.

The wine was, of course, the newly marketed and highly successful Renault-Bardow, and a multitude of toasts were given after glasses etched with the royal crest had been filled.

Dessert, which Emily and Charlane politely refused, then congratulated each other on their willpower, was creamy caramel dribbled over egg custard.

The meal was concluded with brandy in waferthin snifters and coffee in delicate china.

None of the MacAllister children had made the trip to the Island of Wilshire. The older ones were in school and were staying with friends, the babies had been, as one of the daddies put it, "farmed out" to close friends who had young children of their own.

Alice smiled as she swept her gaze down the long table, seeing loving glances being exchanged between the various couples.

They were all treating this journey like a second honeymoon, she mused, with no thoughts of responsibilities surrounding their children or even what to cook for dinner. Therefore, the smoldering desire evident in Brent's eyes every time he looked at her was going, thank goodness, unnoticed.

"Shall we adjourn to the drawing room?" King Chester said finally.

"My dear brother," Charlane said, laughing, "you sound so pompous and stuffy, like something out of a Victorian novel."

King Chester roared with laughter. "I've always wanted to say that. It's awful, isn't it? Although it's a rather kingly thing. I usually say, 'Let's find some more comfortable chairs.' Royal antiques are all very well and good, but they're murder on the backside.''

With a great deal of laughter, the group followed the king out of the dining room, down the hallway and into a large but welcoming room where a stack of presents had been placed by a love seat. The other sofas and easy chairs were soon filled, and the remainder of the family, including Alice and Brent, settled on the floor where they were cushioned by deep, plush carpeting. Maggie and Devon sat on the love seat next to the gifts.

"Open the one from Tr…Alice first," Forrest said, pointing to the pile of presents. "It's the one in the blue paper with the white doves. I'll pop a seam if I have to keep silent any longer. Go ahead, Maggie, Devon…blue paper, white doves.''

"My goodness, Uncle Forrest," Maggie said, "you're making this gift sound so mysterious.'' She leaned over to retrieve the present. "Mmm. Should I make some guesses first as to what it is?''

"No," Forrest said, laughing. "I won't survive that. Just open it, Maggie.''

Alice reached for Brent's hand and gripped it tightly as she felt a bevy of butterflies swoosh suddenly into her very full stomach.

"What's the mystery about your gift?'' Brent

whispered in her ear, then paused. "I don't mean to be picky, but you're breaking my hand."

"Oh. I'm sorry." Alice released Brent's hand and drew a steadying breath. "I'm just so nervous because my gift is—"

"Oh, it's beautiful. Look at those colors," Maggie said, holding the painting at arm's length. "Isn't it an exquisite seascape, Devon?"

"It certainly is," he said, nodding. "It will have a place of honor in our home when we get it built. Do you know the artist personally, Alice? Whoever signed it at the bottom with that distinctive *A?*"

"Go over there, sweetheart," Forrest said to Alice. "Tell them who painted it and let Maggie give you a hug, which she'll definitely want to do."

"But…" Alice started, then looked quickly at Brent, who had a puzzled expression on his face. "I…oh, dear, now the spotlight is on me and…" She got to her feet. "All right, Dad, I'm going, but only for a minute."

"Mark that down somewhere, Jillian," Forrest said, chuckling. "Trip actually did as she was told by her creaky old father."

"Alice," Jillian said. "Honey, do remember that our daughter's name is Alice."

Alice stood in front of the presents stacked by the love seat so she wouldn't have her back to the others in the room. Everyone was looking at her intently.

"Maggie, Devon," Alice said, her voice not quite steady as the butterflies continued to flutter, "I'm so pleased you like the picture because I... What I mean is, the signature that consists of that flowing *A* is... I realize, Maggie, that you had no idea that I..."

"Father races to the rescue," Forrest said. "You're a tad rattled, baby girl." He paused. "Maggie, Devon, you are holding a painting produced by none other than the next artist of fame and fortune who is, I am extremely proud to add, going to have an invitation-only showing of her work at *the* most prestigious of Ventura's galleries in the very near future, and who—"

"Cut to the chase, dear," Jillian said, patting her husband on the knee.

"Oh." Forrest got to his feet. "May I present my daughter, the artist, who painted that fantastic picture... Ms. Alice MacAllister."

Maggie jumped to her feet, still holding the painting. "Oh, my gosh. Oh, Trip...excuse me...Alice, *you* did this? Oh. Oh! This is unbelievable. You're going to have a private showing of your work at... Oh, my gracious, this is so exciting."

"Well, now, let's have a closer look at this," King Chester said, getting up and crossing the room. He was followed by Charlane, Byron and Maggie's parents. "That is a truly marvelous piece of work. You are a very talented young woman, Alice."

"Thank you," she said.

"I hope you have an agent," Charlane said, staring at the painting. "You are obviously on your way to having a brilliant, highly successful career, Alice, and you must be certain that no one takes advantage of you."

"Yes, I do have an excellent agent," Alice said.

The others in the room began to converge on the area by the love seat, everyone seeming to be talking at once about Alice's work, how none of them had known her amazing secret, how proud they all were of her, and on and on. Alice attempted to get a glimpse of Brent, but couldn't see him through the crush of the chattering families.

"What are you going to wear to your showing, Alice?" Jessica said. "It has to be an absolutely stunning dress, befitting someone of your talent. Plus, there will be reporters and photographers there, I'm sure, and the dress has to be just perfect."

"Oh, well, my agent came to my loft," Alice

said, "and selected what she thought would be best and... Please, enough of this. I sincerely thank you all for your enthusiasm and support. It means more to me that I can ever begin to tell you, but we're supposed to be watching Maggie and Devon open their gifts."

Alice snatched up a present from the floor and extended it to Maggie, who had no choice but to lean the painting against the side of the love seat and accept the gift. Everyone returned to their seats, still exclaiming over Alice's marvelous surprise.

Alice started back to where she had been sitting on the floor with Brent, only to discover that he was no longer there. A chill swept through her, then disappeared in the next instant as she saw him leaning one shoulder against the far wall, his arms folded over his chest.

As a chorus of oohs and aahs filled the air when Maggie revealed the gift she had unwrapped, Alice hurried to where Brent was standing, her step slowing slightly as she saw the deep frown on his face.

"Did you get tired of sitting on the floor?" Alice said when she reached Brent.

"No," he said, no hint of a smile on his face. "That was quite a bombshell you just laid on everyone, Alice. You're a very talented artist. But you know that, don't you? After all you have an agent, you're going to have a private showing of your work. Oh, yes, ma'am, that is a heavy-duty secret agenda you've been keeping under wraps. From everyone. From me.''

''I was going to tell you about it when we were alone earlier today,'' Alice said, ''but…well…we had other things on our minds… But now you know and I thought you would be pleased, Brent, but obviously you're not.''

''Pleased?'' he said, pushing himself off the wall and planting his hands on his hips. He glanced quickly at the group of people in the room. ''This isn't the place. Come outside into the garden.''

Brent spun around and strode away. Alice stared at him for a long moment, her mind racing with confusion and a cold sense of dread, then hurried after him.

Brent was very angry, she thought frantically. She had seen the fury in the depths of his eyes and…and a flicker of hurt, raw pain. Oh, dear heaven, why was he reacting this way?

Outside on a path that led through a magnificent rose garden, Brent turned to face Alice, a muscle jumping in his jaw.

''I've been such a fool, it's a crime,'' he said, none too quietly. ''It was all there right in front of me and I was such a besotted idiot I didn't see it.

The loft with the light an artist would need to work, the smell of paint, the fact that you were living beyond the means of a waitress.'' He shook his head. ''My God, I'm stupid.''

''Brent, please, listen to me,'' Alice said, placing one hand on his forearm.

Brent jerked his arm and Alice pulled back her hand, realizing with horror that he didn't even want her to touch him.

''Here was a woman,'' he said, his voice gritty, ''that I didn't even think existed in this world. An honest woman, one who was exactly what she presented herself to be. A woman with no secret agenda to blindside me with when it was too late to protect my heart. What…a…joke.

''You used me, Alice MacAllister, to fill your idle hours until you could launch your big-time career in the artistic community. You used me.''

''No!'' she said. ''That's not true. I…''

''Why did you have to take it so far?'' he continued, pain and anger ringing in his voice. ''Did it give you a rush, a real kick, to accept my proposal of marriage, to tell me how much you love me, when you knew damn well you were just playing games?''

''I *do* love you, Brent,'' Alice said, struggling against threatening tears. ''I do.''

"Yeah, right," he said with a bitter bark of laughter. "You're going back to Ventura after Devon and Maggie's wedding to count down the days until the private showing of your work. You have an agent to take care of details even down to picking out the dress you're to wear at the gallery on the big night. Your focus is on your career, not on me, on us, on what we supposedly were going to have together. Here. On the Island of Wilshire."

"I'm going to paint here, on your island and…"

"Ah, give it a rest. I've come out of the ether, Alice. You'll have to find another toy to play with until you become one of the rich and famous. After your showing there will be interviews, talk shows, photographers wanting to take pictures of where you live and work. Between your painting and the publicity circuit, you'll be a busy little bee, won't you?"

"I…" Alice started, then stopped speaking. She hadn't given a moment's thought to what might transpire after the showing. She'd been concentrating on the hope that her work would sell that night, hadn't considered what would follow if the show was a success. "I…"

"Gotcha, lady. Your silence speaks volumes. You can't deny a word of what I'm saying. You're guilty as charged," Brent said, a rough edge to his voice. "What are you thinking right now? That maybe you should go on a big shopping spree so you'll be dressed to the nines for the cameras?"

"Brent, no, stop this," Alice said, tears spilling onto her cheeks. "You're wrong. You're drawing conclusions that aren't true. You don't understand."

"Oh, I understand perfectly. You're a master at keeping secrets. Hell, you wouldn't even tell me what your grandfather gave you as your special present. Did he know about your dandy agenda? What was the gift? A really expensive set of paints?"

"No, it was a pewter picture frame, and he requested that I... That's not important now. Oh, Brent, please, will you just hear me out? Listen to me. Please."

"No," he said, taking a step backward, his voice suddenly very low and very weary-sounding. "I don't want to hear any more lies. But you'd better listen up to everything I'm about to say. This is Maggie and Devon's special time. Nothing, nor no one, is going to put a damper on it.

"In front of the families, we'll fake it, act like the romantic lovebirds they believe us to be. Privately? Stay away from me, Alice. Just stay the hell away from me.

"I had been counting the hours and minutes until you would arrive here. Now I'm doing the same thing in reverse, ticking them off until you're on that plane and off my island, out of my life, my world. My heart? That will take some time, a long time, but I'll do it. I'll forget you even exist."

"Oh, dear God," Alice said, pressing her trembling fingertips to her lips as a sob caught in her throat. "Brent, no."

"Tell the families I wasn't feeling well," he said. "I can't handle putting on a false front tonight. But starting tomorrow we do award-winning performances. Got that? Sure you do. You've had a lot of experience pretending to be something you're not. Just look at it as another game you're playing."

"Brent, please," Alice said, dashing the tears from her cheeks. "You're wrong. About everything. I didn't tell you or my family sooner about my dream, my painting, because I was terribly frightened, so afraid of baring my soul, being vulnerable, after so many years of hiding behind my walls. I was terrified of being Alice, instead of Trip.

"Oh, don't you see? As Trip I knew how to protect myself, keep everyone at arm's length, and I needed time to gather the courage to be…to be Alice. You helped give me the strength to do that,

Brent. I was Alice in Wonderland to you. I became Alice, the woman, for me.

"I *do* love you with all my heart," she added, tears now streaming unnoticed down her face and along her neck. "I want to marry you, create the miracle of our babies with you, live with you here, on the Island of Wilshire, until death parts us. You've got to believe me, Brent. *Please.* I'll paint endless pictures *here,* be so content on your beautiful island and—"

"Until the telephone rings," Brent said, his voice flat, "and your agent tells you about the next talk show you're scheduled to be on, or the tour she's arranged for you to promote your work. Then off you'll fly without a backward glance. I don't call that loving me, Alice. Not even close.

"And our babies? Hell. You'll find a hundred excuses to postpone starting our family because, after all, your career, your damnable secret agenda, comes first.

"No, your idea of love doesn't match up with mine. We're not soul mates as I believed us to be."

"Brent..." Alice said, then stopped and shook her head, tears choking off her words.

"The game is over," he said. "You had a good laugh at my expense and now you're on your way to the spotlight of fame and all the perks that go with it.

"You don't need me to say you should enjoy yourself, do you? That's been your plan all along. In fact, you don't need me for a damn thing."

"Brent?" Charlane called in the distance. "Are you out there? I realize that you and Alice want some time to be together, but we do have guests, dear."

"I'm sorry, Mother," Brent yelled. "But I'm not feeling very well. Please extend my apologies to everyone."

"I can't go back in there," Alice whispered. "They'll all know I've been crying and…I just can't."

"Fine," Brent said tersely, "I'll bail you out tonight, but remember that starting tomorrow we put on the show they expect to see."

Alice nodded jerkily, then another sob escaped from her lips.

"Mother?" Brent called. "Are you still there?"

"Yes, I'm here. Do you need a doctor, Brent?"

"No, no, I'm just going to hit the sack. Listen, Alice is exhausted. Jet leg and all that. She's going on to her room now. I'm sure everyone will understand that it's been a long day for her. They're all probably as tired as she is, come to think of it."

"All right," Charlane said. "Sleep well. Both of you. I'll suggest we make an early evening of it in here for the sake of the travelers. See you both tomorrow."

"Good night, Mother," Brent called, then looked at Alice. "Goodbye, Alice in Wonderland. Hey, that was a perfect name for you all along, and I didn't know it at the time. Alice in Wonderland doesn't exist. She's a fantasy from a fairy tale. In the real world, there is no Alice in Wonderland. There never was."

Brent turned and strode way, disappearing in moments into the darkness. Alice reached out one trembling hand toward him, then dropped it back to her side. She stumbled forward and sank onto a cement bench with intricate scrollwork on the top.

Wrapping her arms around her stomach, she rocked back and forth, sobbing openly, as she was consumed by the greatest pain and heartache she had ever known.

This wasn't happening, she thought frantically. She was in the midst of a devastating nightmare. She would wake up and find herself snuggled close to Brent in his bed in the cottage where they'd shared exquisitely beautiful lovemaking. He would tell her they had to hurry or they'd be late for the first-night-on-the-island welcoming dinner in the castle and...

Alice drew a shuddering breath, then a chill swept through her, touching her heart, mind and soul.

No, this wasn't a nightmare formed by images while sleeping. This was the nightmare of reality. She had demolished her protective walls, had emerged as Alice, had fallen in love and given her heart to Brent to have and to hold, to love and to cherish.

And he'd crushed it.

He viewed her as a scheming, devious, game-playing woman, who had used him to fill idle hours as she waited for the launching of her artistic career.

He despised her.

Brent didn't believe in her, or in her love for him. Not anymore. He'd flung hateful accusations at her that had felt like physical blows, shattering her into a million pieces. Like Humpty-Dumpty, Alice in Wonderland could never be put back together again.

Alice got to her feet, swayed for a moment, then steadied.

But Alice, the woman? she thought. She'd have to survive, move forward. Somehow. The alternative was to rebuild the walls and become Trip again, and she didn't want to do that. No, not that.

She was Alice.

She would remain Alice.

Alone and lonely, having loved and lost the most magnificent man who walked this earth. The man she would love until she drew her last breath. The man she would ache for, miss so much, cry tears for during the bleak, dark hours of the night for a long, long time.

Chapter Eleven

The next morning the MacAllisters were treated to a tour of the island while riding in a long wagon with padded seats and pulled by a team of eight sleek horses.

To Alice's utmost relief, none of the Bardows were at breakfast, although a cheerful Charlane arrived at the castle in time to accompany the group on the tour.

When Maggie commented on Alice's puffy, red-rimmed eyes, she popped on a pair of sunglasses and told her cousin that she was apparently allergic to something that was in bloom that she wasn't accustomed to.

"That's certainly understandable, Alice," Charlane said. "There's a multitude of flowers here that aren't grown in Ventura. You'll build up a tolerance for them in time, never fear." She smiled brightly. "Providing, of course, that you're in close proximity to the blossoms for a, shall we say, extended period."

Alice managed to produce a small smile, then climbed into the wagon and smothered a weary sigh.

Charlane Bardow, she thought, was about as subtle as a rock. She was making it clear that she fully expected Alice to marry Brent and live on Wilshire, which would solve the nagging little problem of being allergic to the flowers growing there.

But that wasn't going to happen, nor was the condition of her less-than-attractive eyes due to being allergic to the plants. She'd wept her way through the long night, dozing from total exhaustion at times, then waking again to cry into her pillow over the heartbreaking loss of her Brent.

Oh, dear heaven, she wanted to go home, Alice thought, as King Chester pointed out things of interest they were passing as the horses plodded along. How was she going to get through the following days without falling apart, dissolving into a puddle of tears and telling everyone that her heart was smashed to smithereens?

Get a grip, she told herself. The only thing that Brent had been right about during his tirade last night was the fact that nothing should spoil Maggie and Devon's special event. She would have to reach deep within herself for the fortitude to produce a cheerful demeanor, not give one clue that anything was wrong.

But, oh, God, how was she going to bear being close to Brent at the scheduled events and pretend they were still madly in love with each other, give everyone the impression that the next wedding on the calendar would be the exchanging of vows between Alice MacAllister and Brent Bardow?

Oh, Brent, Alice thought, blinking away sudden tears. She loved him so much. If only there was something that she could do, or say, to make him believe in her again. But there wasn't. It was hopeless. It was over.

"Alice," Jillian whispered, leaning close to her daughter in the seat they were sharing.

"Yes, Mother?" Alice said, turning her head while being very grateful that she'd remembered to pack the sunglasses she intended to wear at every opportunity.

"There are bumps in the road of love," Jillian said quietly, so only Alice could hear, "in every romance since the beginning of time. The true test of love is not to give up, not leave that road because it's painful for you at the moment."

"I never said——" Alice started.

"I'm your mother, my darling," Jillian said gently. "I know you're very unhappy right now, although your being allergic to the flowers number was very inventive. Only a woman who is deeply in love would have cried as you have. Don't give up on what you and Brent have together just because, for whatever reason, you two have hit a rocky spot in the road."

"I have no choice but to accept that it's over," Alice said, struggling against her tears. "Brent truly believes that I..." She shook her head. "I can't talk about it or I'll... I promise I won't do anything to spoil things for Maggie and Devon. That's the only thing that Brent and I are in accord about."

Jillian patted her daughter's knee. "I understand. But do remember that I'm here for you. Think about what I said, too. True love can weather many storms."

"Not *this* storm," Alice said, smiling slightly. "This is a hurricane, a tornado and a typhoon all wrapped up in a devastating package that has destroyed what Brent and I had beyond repair. I—"

"To your right," King Chester said, bringing Alice and Jillian back to attention, "as far as the eye can see are Brent's vineyards. Devon handles the paperwork, the management end of things. Brent works side by side with his employees in the fields. Brent is a man of the earth, a nurturer, who gives his heart and soul to what he loves. We're extremely proud of what he's accomplished for all of us here on Wilshire."

Yes, Alice thought, reflecting on King Chester's words. That was how he had loved her, would have loved the children they would have created together. Totally. Absolutely. A man of the earth, who worked so hard, so diligently for what he believed in and cherished. Oh, what they would have had as husband and wife, father and mother, partners, soul mates.

Oh, what would have been, but would never be.

That afternoon a final fitting of the bridesmaids' dresses took place in one of the multitude of huge bedrooms in the castle.

Maggie had chosen rainbow colors for her attendants: Jessica in pink, Emily wearing yellow, and to Alice's dismay, her dress was a lighter shade of Brent's blue eyes.

The seamstress, Ruth, was a wonder, had made the dresses from nothing more than Maggie's descriptions of her cousin's figures. Shoes had been dyed to match the material and only the hems to the dresses were yet to be done.

Emily's dress, however, had to be taken in as she had shed another six pounds during the month since the royal family had left Ventura.

"I'm sorry to cause you extra work," Emily said to Ruth, who was pinning the dress, "but I'm personally thrilled that I'm actually sticking to my diet. And this time I intend to keep the weight off permanently. I'd hate to add up how many pounds I've lost and gained over the years."

"It's no problem to fix this," Ruth said. "But I hope you don't get as skinny as your sisters. Women need to be women, not sticks."

"Hear, hear," Jessica said, laughing. "Bring on some chocolate."

"It's true," Ruth said. "You need meat on your bones so you can nurse many healthy babies."

"My baby days are over," Emily said, smiling. "My son is nearly as tall as I am already. I'm overdue to be a stick."

"You have many years left to have babies,"

Ruth said, frowning. "Why would you say your baby days are over, Emily?"

"Because," Emily said, suddenly serious, "that's…that's the way I want it. No men in my life, no babies in my future. I'm just creating a home for me and my son, running my own business. That's all I need." She smiled again. "Now, Jessica and Tr…Alice are a different story. Talk to them about putting meat on their bones so they can nurse those babies you're speaking of."

Jessica laughed. "All in good time, Emily. Do remember that I became an instant mother to Tessa when I married Daniel. One in diapers is enough to handle at the moment. There. I'm off the hook."

"For now," Emily said. "That leaves our sister Alice, the Stick. From what we all saw when we arrived at the airport here, Brent is obviously thinking about more than just grapes."

Alice sent a frantic look to her mother, and Jillian got quickly to her feet from where she was sitting on a love seat.

"I believe Emily's dress needs to be nipped in just a tad more at the waist," she said, crossing the room. "What do you think?" She swept her gaze over the other women in the room, prompting opinions to be offered.

Thank you, Mother, Alice thought, sinking onto

an easy chair. How very sad this charade was. She was once again pretending to be someone she wasn't, keeping the secret of her broken heart from those who loved her unconditionally. But she had to do it this way for Maggie's sake.

Somehow, *somehow,* when she saw Brent at dinner that night she'd appear carefree and happy, would stay close to his side, not give even one hint that there was anything wrong between them. Somehow.

"There he is," Charlane said as Brent strode into the dining room that evening. "Late, per usual."

"Sorry," Brent said, sliding onto his chair next to Alice. "I had a long-distance call at the last minute, but I'm here now. Bring on the food."

"And hungry, per usual," Byron said, chuckling.

"Hello, sweet person," Brent said. He kissed Alice on the cheek but didn't look into her eyes. "Did you have a nice day?"

"Yes," she said, fiddling with her napkin, "it was lovely."

"Good," Brent said. "Ah, here comes the soup. I am one famished man."

How on earth was she going to choke down this food? Alice thought miserably. Brent was sitting right there next to her, only a handful of inches away, yet the distance she could feel between them was like a deep chasm that could not be crossed.

She could feel, actually feel, the vibrant heat emanating from Brent's powerful body, could smell his musky aftershave and the lingering aroma of fresh soap from his shower.

Her cheek where he'd kissed her, she thought, forcing herself not to place her fingertips there, was still tingling with warmth, evoking memories of the lovemaking they'd shared.

"Didn't she, Alice?" Emily asked, snapping Alice back to attention.

"Pardon me?"

"The seamstress, Ruth," Emily said. "She was a delightful woman who decided that Jessica and you were built like sticks and needed to fatten up some so you could nurse your healthy, bouncing babies."

"I…" Alice said.

"Some women would rather focus on their careers than have babies," Brent said.

Oh, Brent, Alice thought, *don't.*

"Well, I intend to have it all," Jessica said. "A career and the roles of wife and mother. It can be done, Brent, if the couple works together."

"Amen to that." Daniel smiled at Jessica.

"We'll be the proof of that pudding, or however that old saying goes."

Brent nodded. "I agree with you, Jessica, but if the woman's career is all-consuming, there isn't room for anything else in her life."

Jessica shrugged. "I suppose you're right, but the same is to be said of the man. The couple has to be in balance, sharing, compromising, knowing when work ends for the day and family focus begins. Daniel might be called out on a case during what might be his usual time to read a story to Tessa, but the foundation is there, is in place, in the big picture of our life together."

"You're to be envied," Brent said. "Not everyone is as fortunate as you and Daniel, Jessica. For some of us, that balance, shall we say, is out of reach."

"Nonsense," Byron said. "No one is pointing a gun at your head, Brent, demanding that you put in the ridiculously long days that you do in the vineyards." He smiled at Alice. "You just haven't had a reason to cut back on your hours in the past. Things change."

"Yes, they do, don't they?" Brent said, a slight edge to his voice. "Sometimes when you least expect it, things change so drastically it knocks you for a loop. Maggie, would you pass me the pepper, please?''

Alice crossed her legs beneath the table and kicked Brent in the calf.

''Ow!'' he said.

''Oh, I'm terribly sorry,'' she said, ever so sweetly. Tit for tat. Brent had gotten in his little zinger, his dig at her, thinking she had no choice but to sit there and take it.

''Yeah, right,'' Brent said, under his breath.

''One should not push a MacAllister beyond the line in the sand.'' Jillian laughed softly.

''Where did that come from?'' Forrest said. ''Am I missing something here? Is this a woman thing I wouldn't understand even if you told me?''

''It certainly is,'' Jillian said, then looked directly at Brent. ''Men can be terribly stubborn at times, get into a mind-set and refuse to budge, won't even entertain the idea that they might be wrong.''

''Some men might do that,'' Brent said, meeting Jillian's gaze. ''I, however, make certain that I have all my data, the facts as they stand, know that I'm right.''

''I'm definitely missing something here,'' Forrest mumbled.

''My, my,'' Alice said, ''this topic is getting very

heavy, isn't it? King Chester, what...what kingly things did you do today?''

As King Chester began to reply, Alice tuned out and breathed a sigh of relief.

Her mother's protective instincts had risen to the fore, she thought, and she'd been ready to go toe-to-toe with Brent, not even knowing the full story of what had destroyed his relationship with her daughter. That was very loving of her mother, but it couldn't continue or the others would pick up on the fact that this was not just dinner chitchat.

Dear heaven, would this meal never end?

During the following days and nights preceding the wedding, the essence of that frantic plea became Alice's mantra.

Would the fancy, women-only tea in the castle garden never end?

Would the shopping trip into the quaint village in the center of Wilshire never end?

Would the agonizing tour of the winery, which was conducted by Brent, never end?

Would the music played by the string quartet that came to the castle to entertain the guests while she was sitting next to Brent on a sofa never end?

Would the formal reception to welcome the multitude of dignitaries arriving from around the world for the wedding never end?

Would the long, lonely nights spent weeping into her pillow never, ever end?

On the morning of the wedding, which was scheduled, by royal tradition, to take place at high noon, Alice woke at dawn and mentally held tight to the knowledge that early tomorrow morning she could go home.

She had to survive the wedding and the long, lavish reception following it today, then this nightmare would be over. Returning to Ventura, she knew, was not going to erase the dark, gloomy cloud that seemed to continually hover over her. But at least she would be home and could, hopefully, get at least some reprieve from her misery as she concentrated on her work.

As sunlight began to fill the lovely bedroom, Alice turned her head on the pillow to look at the beautiful bridesmaid's dress that hung on a padded hanger on an antique clothes tree.

Her cousin Maggie, Alice mused, was going to marry her prince today. It was a fairy tale come true. Maggie would be a princess and someday a queen. She and Devon were so very much in love that an aura of sunshine seemed to encase them whenever they were together.

Maggie was Cinderella, and Snow White and all the others in the whimsical stories of handsome princes claiming their brides for all time.

"And me?" Alice said aloud.

She was still dumb Alice in Wonderland, falling through the hole and tumbling down, down, down, because she'd been stupid enough to follow some idiotic rabbit who couldn't even manage to get to an appointment on time.

There was no handsome prince waiting for *her*. There was no happy ending for *her*. There was no longer magnificent Brent Bardow in love with her.

Alice drew a wobbly breath.

Stop feeling sorry for yourself, Alice MacAllister, she thought firmly. Enough of this pity party trip she was on. But, oh, dear heaven, she was just so...so sad. What a tiny little word. Three letters. Sad. But it spoke volumes with its chilling truth that totally consumed her.

And she had no one to blame but herself.

"Just like the white rabbit," Alice whispered. "I was late, too late, for the most important date with destiny of my entire life."

Alice looked again at the bridesmaid's dress.

"Always the bridesmaid," she said, then sniffled. "But I'll never, ever be Brent's bride."

In the groom's room in the church, Devon looked at his watch, stared into space, then glanced at his watch again as he realized he hadn't registered the time in his jumbled mind.

"Fifteen minutes," he said. "Why did they stick us in this room so soon?"

Brent leaned one shoulder against the wall and crossed his arms over his chest. "So you could have your nervous breakdown and get over it, cousin," he said. "Cripes, Devon, calm down. You're going to feel like the jerk of the century if you pass out cold on your face at the altar. Get a grip, man."

"Grip," Devon said, nodding jerkily. "I'm getting it. The grip. Here I am. Getting a grip. Brent, I'm about to be married."

Brent nodded slowly. "That's the plan." He paused and frowned. "This isn't a case of cold feet I'm witnessing here, is it?"

"How can you even suggest such a thing?" Devon said, none too quietly. "This is the happiest day of my life. I'm marrying my Maggie. My beautiful, sweet, wonderful princess, the woman of my dreams. I just wish there weren't five hundred people out there waiting for me to mess up what I'm supposed to say, when it's my turn to say what I'm supposed to say, when I say what I'm supposed to... Ah, hell, I'm losing it.''

"Big time," Brent said, shaking his head. "Look, try this. Tell yourself there is no one in that church except you and Maggie. Just the two of you. Focus on Maggie, on how much you love her, on the fantastic future you're going to have together. She'll be your wife, Devon, your soul mate and partner for life and...''

An achy sensation gripped Brent's throat and he stopped speaking.

Ah, Alice, he thought. Everything he was saying should be describing what they would share, what they would have together.

He loved her. He despised her.

He couldn't bear the thought of her leaving Wilshire tomorrow. He never wanted to see her again.

She was everything he had ever hoped to find in a woman, a wife. She was nothing close to being who he'd believed her to be.

"Hey, Brent?" Devon said. "What's wrong? You suddenly look like you lost your best friend.''

"Got it in one, cousin," Brent said. "Forget it. I'm fine. You're the one who is coming unglued. Here. We're supposed to put these dorky boutonniere things in our lapels. Somebody nuts thought up all this junk. Why do guys need a dinky flower on their coat so they can get married?'' He opened a white florist box that was sitting on a small table. "Oops."

"Oops?" Devon said. "Don't say 'oops' when I'm hanging on by a thread here.'' He crossed the room and looked in the box. "That's a corsage, Brent. You know, the mother-of-the-bride thing, or something. There should be two boutonnieres in that box and…oh, this is just great. Dandy. Perfect. I can't get married to my Maggie because some idiot lost my boutonniere.''

"Chill," Brent said, placing his hands on Devon's shoulders. "The boxes got switched, that's all. I'll go around to the other side through the back hallway and I betcha a buck the women are in the bride's room, or whatever the hell you call it, ready to trade flowers. Okay? Say 'okay, Brent.'''

"Okay, Brent," Devon said.

"Good boy," Brent said, patting Devon on the cheek. "I'll be back in a flash. Try not to have a complete mental collapse while I'm gone."

"Okay, Brent."

"Hopeless," Brent said, then snatched up the box and left the room.

Brent strode along the narrow, dimly lit corridor, then stopped suddenly in his tracks, his heart thundering so wildly it caused an actual physical pain in his chest.

There she was, he thought hazily. Alice. She was coming toward him, a vision of loveliness in a beautiful blue dress. There she was, walking down the aisle to take her place at his side, to repeat the sacred vows with him that would unite them in marriage. There she was. His bride. His Alice of wonder. And he loved her so damn much.

Look at us, Brent thought. As the decades went by and their love grew even deeper and richer, they would gaze into each other's eyes and say the words…look at us, after all these years together, look at you, still pretty as a picture, look at me, still crazy over you.

Oh, God, Alice.

She stopped several feet away from him.

"Brent," Alice said, her voice trembling, "the flowers, this box has the boutonnieres that you and Devon… Do you have a corsage in that box you're holding?"

Do you, Brent, take this woman to be your wife, to have and to hold from this day forward, Brent's mind hummed from a faraway place.

"I do," he said, emotion ringing in his voice.

To love and to cherish, Alice thought hazily, in

sickness and in health, for richer, for poorer, forever, forever, forever...

Oh, Brent.

"I do," Alice whispered.

They walked slowly forward, closing the distance between them, looking deep into each other's eyes, hearts racing, breaths catching, unshed tears causing eyes to sting.

It was magic, their magic, returned to them, encasing them in a mist of splendor and joy and love so intense it was a nearly palpable entity weaving around and through them, chasing away the chill with a warmth that touched their hearts and souls.

"Brent!" Devon called in the distance. "Come on. It's time. It's time."

Brent jerked and dropped the box he was holding. He leaned down, snatched it from the floor and shoved it at Alice, forcing her to accept it.

"Brent?" she said, searching his face as she drew a wobbly breath.

"No," he said, a rough edge to his voice as he took the other box from her hand. "Don't say anything to me, Alice. Not anything...except...goodbye."

The wedding ceremony was breathtaking.

Sunlight streamed through the stained-glass windows of the enormous church, creating a wondrous rainbow of colors to cascade over the bride and groom. They spoke their vows with voices steady and sure as they pledged their love to each other for eternity. Matching rings were slipped onto fingers as visible signs of what was in their hearts, minds and souls.

As Maggie and Devon turned to be introduced as husband and wife to the multitude of witnesses, tears flowed freely from those who saw the glorious radiance of their love for each other.

Tears shimmered, too, in the eyes of Alice and Brent, but theirs were born of heartache for what would never be for them.

Chapter Twelve

As dawn crept quietly above the horizon the next morning with muted colors that grew more vibrant as they began to fill the sky, Alice stood hidden in the trees by Brent's cottage.

She'd been there an hour already, having arrived in the dark, and was chilled through, the slacks and lightweight sweater she'd chosen to wear during the flight home not warm enough for the crisp night air.

During the seemingly endless hours of the night, she'd decided that this was what she wanted, needed to do. It would probably mean nothing to Brent, but it was very, very important to her.

Giving up on attempting to sleep, she'd showered, dressed, then packed her suitcases. Feeling like a sneak thief, she'd crept down the stairs and out the front doors of the castle.

With only the stars to light the path, she made her way to Brent's cottage without a wrong turn, as though she had been there a hundred times, instead of only once.

It was as though, she thought, her heart was leading the way to the man she loved beyond measure.

A shiver coursed through Alice as a breeze rustled the leaves on the trees, then her breath caught as she saw the glow of light suddenly appear behind the curtains of the cottage. Having no idea what time he usually started his day, she had come early so she'd be certain that Brent had left the cottage and she could complete her mission.

Fifteen minutes later, the door to the cottage opened and Alice almost forgot to breathe as Brent stepped outside, clad only in faded jeans riding low on his hips.

Even from where she stood hidden in the trees, she could see that his hair was damp from a morning shower, and for a moment she was convinced she could actually smell his wonderful aroma of soap and fresh air. He was sipping from a mug, and he scanned the sky to gauge the weather for the day.

Alice drank in the sight of Brent, memorizing every detail of him, etching each indelibly in her mind. Tears stung the back of her eyes and she blinked them away, refusing to cry, wondering when she would have no more tears left.

Brent tossed the last of the coffee on the ground, then his shoulders slumped and he dropped his chin to his bare chest that rose, then fell from a deep sigh.

Oh, God, Alice thought, pressing the trembling fingertips of one hand to her lips, Brent looked so defeated, so exhausted. So very, very sad. *She* had done this to him, and the weight of her guilt was crushing.

''I'm so sorry, my love,'' she whispered, unable to stop the tears that spilled onto her cheeks.

Brent went back into the cottage and shut the door, emerging ten minutes later fully dressed. He strode away and disappeared in the opposite direction from where Alice was standing.

She waited another twenty minutes to be absolutely certain that Brent wouldn't return, then moved from her hiding place and ran to the cottage. She hesitated, then with a firm resolve, opened the door and entered the little house.

A short time later when Alice stepped into the entryway of the castle, she mentally moaned when she saw her family coming down the stairs.

Great timing, she thought dryly. She knew that an early breakfast had been scheduled so they could make their flight, but had hoped she'd be back in her room before the others emerged from theirs and it would appear as though she had followed the same plan as the group. Oh, well, bring on the bare lightbulb. She was about to be grilled by the pros regarding what she had been up to.

"Good morning, sweetheart," Jillian said as she crossed the entryway.

"Hi," Alice said weakly. "I…"

"I'm ready for some of those spicy little sausages," Forrest said. "I wonder if we could get the recipe for those, Jillian." He glanced at Alice. "Coming, kiddo? The next meal we'll have will be airplane food, so let's fill up while we're here."

"I…" Alice said, raising one finger in the air.

Jessica winked at her sister as she and Daniel went past Alice, then Emily beamed at her. The others strolled by, and Alice was the recipient of knowing smiles and smothered laughter.

Whatever, Alice thought, mentally throwing up her hands as she followed the family. They all believed, apparently, that she'd had a private, romantic farewell with Brent and they were going to leave it at that, no doubt feeling very sophisticated with their acceptance of her torrid affair with Brent Bardow.

My heart is smashed to smithereens, people, Alice yelled in her mind. *I'm a walking, talking, crying jag.*

Alice sniffled and six members of her family looked at her questioningly.

"Allergies," she mumbled.

"Mmm," Jillian said.

Alice poked at her food as everyone ate and chatted about the beautiful wedding of the day before. Maggie and Devon were off on a two-week honeymoon to a destination they had refused to reveal, and Forrest started taking bets on where they had gone.

Finally giving up any attempt to choke down a bite, Alice pushed her plate away and sipped her coffee. Everyone looked up as a man entered the dining room, handed a note to King Chester, then hurried away. The king read the message, then nodded.

"This is from Brent," he said. "He has things

to take care of at the vineyard this morning that need his personal attention and won't be able to see you off at the plane. He wishes you all a good journey.''

A chill swept through Alice and she set her cup back in the saucer with a shaking hand.

Brent couldn't even bear to see her one last time, she thought miserably. She'd not only destroyed his love for her, she'd pushed him all the way to actually hating the very sight of her. So many hopes and dreams, so very many, were gone...forever.

Charlane and Byron had come to the castle for the farewell breakfast, and Byron shook his head when he heard the message his son had sent.

''Brent works too hard,'' Byron said. ''We discussed that the other evening at dinner, remember? The fact that some people are too focused on their work, their careers. I thought he might be listening to me, but apparently he wasn't.''

''I...I don't believe he was referring to himself,'' Alice said quietly. ''He...never mind. It's not important. Now.'' She cringed as she glanced around the table and saw that everyone was looking at her. ''What I mean is...um...well, I...''

''What you're saying,'' Jillian said, ''is that it often takes time for change. Right, dear?''

''Right,'' Alice said quickly.

"Oh," Byron said, nodding. "Well, that makes sense, I guess. There's hope for that boy yet. He'll get his priorities straight."

"Hear, hear," Charlane said, smiling at Alice.

Brent already had his priorities straight, Alice thought. His first order of business was to erase her from his mind *and* his heart just as quickly as he possibly could.

Late that night Brent entered his cottage, stumbling slightly from total exhaustion. He'd pushed his body to the maximum and beyond the entire day with the hope that he would be so tired he would finally be able to stop thinking and just sleep, blank his mind and sleep.

He snapped on the small lamp by the bed as he tugged his filthy shirt free of his jeans, unbuttoned it and dropped it to the floor. As he unsnapped his grimy jeans, his attention was caught by a tissue-wrapped package propped against one of the pillows on the bed.

Sinking onto the edge of the bed, he frowned as he picked up the parcel, then tore away the paper, his eyes widening as what was inside was revealed.

"The pewter frame," he said aloud. "The one that Alice's grandfather gave her as her secret present. Why did she give something this special to me now?''

He sighed in confusion, then directed his attention to the painting within the frame, his breath catching as he stared at the portrait of Alice. His heart began to beat in a wild tempo and a roaring noise echoed in his ears as he drank in the sight of Alice's face, her eyes, the soft smile on her lips.

His hold on the frame tightened as his gaze stayed riveted on the self-portrait Alice had painted.

This woman, his thoughts racing, is in love. Deeply, intensely in love, and she had the glow of knowing she was loved in return. It was all there for him to see, in this portrait, in this picture that Alice had painted of herself and had now given to him.

This was the truth. This was real. This was Alice in Wonderland, whom he had come to love beyond measure. This was his future.

''Dear God,'' he whispered hoarsely, ''what have I done? Oh, my beloved Alice, what have I done to us?''

Alice entered the loft with her agent close on her heels. Alice sank onto the sofa with a weary sigh, leaned her head on the top and closed her eyes.

''That's it. That's all,'' Alice said. ''I'm done.

I've smiled so much in the three weeks since I've been back that my face is frozen in phony form.''

Delores laughed and sat down in an easy chair opposite the sofa.

"You did beautifully today," she said. "The TV cameras love you, Alice. I have videos of all the other talk shows you've done up and down the coast and you're a natural in front of the cameras.''

"The cameras love me?" Alice said, not moving or opening her eyes. "Hooray for the cameras. What I want is for *people* to love my work, Delores. That's what is important."

"Work they won't know about unless we get the word out about it," Delores said. "Let's see, you've done the talk shows, the radio call-in bit, been interviewed for the newspaper, plus that classy art magazine and—"

"Don't click off anymore on that list," Alice said. "I'm exhausted enough without mentally reliving it all." She raised her head and looked at Delores. "You've done a marvelous job as my agent, you really have. I know you've made an arrangement with the gallery that anything that sells during the private showing is to be left hanging there for a week, plus they have the extra paintings not being seen that first night ready to display.

"But, Delores? I've discovered something about

myself during these three weeks. When someone I know brought up the fact that I would be doing this sort of publicity I was taken off guard because I just hadn't given it any thought. But now I've lived it and I definitely don't like it, not one little bit.''

Delores shrugged. ''Some people do, some don't. It just depends on who you are.''

Alice sat up straighter on the sofa. ''That's my point. I really know now who I am in regard to this arena of publicity, public appearances, the whole nine yards. It's *not* who I am. I don't like the limelight, the personal questions, the prying. I can't, won't, do this again, Delores. Maybe it will mean I won't sell as many paintings in the future, but I want to be honest with you about this. If you'd prefer not to be my agent because I'm being uncooperative—''

''Whoa, sweetie,'' Delores said, raising both hands. ''I'm not going anywhere. You're stuck with me. You've been a real trouper during this godawful schedule I set up for you.'' She shrugged. ''That is that. No problem.''

''My art will speak for me, reflect who I am,'' Alice said. ''That's all that matters.''

''And that's fine, just fine,'' Delores said, getting to her feet. ''You're going to have a long and successful career, Ms. MacAllister, and you don't have to suffer through any more cameras falling in love with you.'' She glanced at her watch. ''I'm off. Don't get up. I can let myself out. You're spending this last week until the show working with the gallery owner on wall placement of your paintings. Right? Right. Okay, sweetie, I'll see you on the big night. It's going to be fabulous. Ta-ta.''

''Ta,'' Alice said, raising one hand as she sank back against the comfy cushions on the sofa. ''Ta.''

See, Brent? she thought, closing her eyes again. It would have all been so perfect.

Except it would never happen.

Because it was too late.

A star-filled sky lit the way as Brent climbed to the top of the hill where he'd stood and watched Alice's plane disappear from view, the place where he'd dreamed of building their home. He'd made this trek every night since he'd discovered the portrait in the pewter frame on his bed after Alice had left the island.

He sank onto the ground and leaned his back against a tree, staring into space.

Night after night, he mused, he came here, hoping to untangle the confusing jumble in his mind and find the answers to the heartbreaking dilemma he was facing. And night after night he accomplished nothing more than chasing his own thoughts in an endless circle in his beleaguered mind.

"And here we go again," he said aloud, his voice weary.

He loved Alice. Alice loved him. He no longer doubted that she truly loved him as much as he loved her. He had only to look at the self-portrait she'd painted to know that was true.

He also now believed that Alice *hadn't* been playing games with him, with his heart, his emotions, to fill her idle hours until her career was launched. No, she had simply been gathering enough inner courage to reveal her hopes and dreams to him, to her family. It hadn't been a secret agenda in the negative sense he'd accused her of, but a secret she'd been too frightened to make known.

Brent bent his knees, propped his elbows on them and made a steeple of his fingers, which he tapped against his lips.

He'd gotten that much straight during his nightly treks, he thought, but couldn't move forward. Still there, like an unbreachable wall standing between him and any future happiness with Alice, was the remainder of the mess in his mind.

Fact. Alice was a very, *very* talented artist, whose career was about to take off like a rocket.

Fact. Careers like hers had to be nurtured, pushed along, with publicity, interviews, public appearances, so that the public could feel a personal link with the artist of the work they were considering buying.

Fact. The necessity of being accessible to her would-be fans and supporters would result in Alice packing a suitcase and flying off to the States whenever her agent said it was time to do it again. Fly off and leave him behind to wander through an empty and lonely house that wouldn't be a home when Alice wasn't there.

Fact. The babies, the miracles, they would have created together with exquisite lovemaking would have to become a forgotten dream because there just wouldn't be room in Alice's schedule for the role of mother. Wearing the hats of wife and successful artist would be all that Alice would be able to handle.

Fact. The scenario he had just repeated...again... just wasn't enough. It was too shallow, too empty too much of the time, to fill him with the happiness that loving and being loved in return should do.

"Ah, damn," Brent said, dragging his hands down his face. "It's hopeless."

He'd just keep on as he was...alone. He'd focus

on the vineyards, start thinking of producing another new, award-winning wine with a heartfelt intensity. Just as in the past when he'd allowed nothing to keep him from achieving his dreams for the excellence of Wilshire wines, he would once again…

Brent stiffened, every muscle in his body tightened to the point of pain, as his heart thundered.

Wait a minute, he thought. Wait just a damn minute here. *He'd allowed nothing to keep him from achieving his dreams.* Yet there he sat, Mr. Holier-than-thou, passing judgment on the woman he loved, deciding that what she had to offer him didn't measure up, when what she was doing was exactly what he had done. *Alice was allowing nothing to keep her from achieving her dreams.*

And she had every right to do that.

"My God," he whispered, his voice hoarse with emotion, "I'm such a selfish jerk. We live our life together, Alice, following only my rules, or forget it. The hell with *your* dreams, *your* hopes, *your* years of dedication to purpose. If they don't match mine, they're not worth squat, lady."

Brent rolled to his feet and stared at the brilliant sky in the direction that Alice's plane had flown when she had left Wilshire. Left *him.*

He had been so wrong, he thought frantically. So

self-centered and wrong. The woman he loved was in love with him and he'd thrown that all away—broken a precious possession that could never be replaced.

So, okay, Alice would have to leave Wilshire to promote her work. But she'd come home. To him.

So, okay, they wouldn't have children. But they'd have each other.

So, okay, it wasn't the existence he'd envisioned them sharing as husband and wife. But it would be theirs, and with compromise, and understanding, and love, they could make it work for them. Forever and ever. Until death parted them.

It was an enormous, terrifying "if"…if Alice would forgive him for the way he'd treated her, the things he'd accused her of that weren't remotely true, if Alice still loved him despite the fact that he had been a rotten human being.

Get a grip, Bardow, get a plan, he told himself. Think. Yes. He'd catch the first plane he could find and fly to Ventura, beg…yes, *beg,* Alice to forgive him. Assure her that he would always be waiting for her to come home when she was finished with whatever promotional tour, showing, whatever, she'd had to attend to. Make her understand, some-how, that they could be happy there as husband and

wife, on Wilshire. They could borrow Maggie and
Devon's kids to play with or something and...

"Oh, God, Alice, please forgive me. Give me,
us, another chance."

Chapter Thirteen

Forrest MacAllister stood in front of the mirror in the bathroom off the master bedroom in the home he shared with Jillian. He muttered under his breath, threw in a few earthy expletives, then...

"Jillian!" he yelled. "I can't get this damnable tie to do what I want it to. It ends up vertical instead of horizontal every time I attempt to... I need some help here. Please, dear wife, come to my rescue."

Jillian laughed and crossed the bedroom to enter the bathroom where Forrest stood scowling.

"We go through this whenever you wear a tuxedo, Forrest," she said, gripping the silky ends of the tie. "I've been coming to your rescue like this for over thirty years."

"I know, I know," he said, "but I always think that this might be the night I'll finally conquer the beast."

"I see," Jillian said, then patted the tie that was now horizontal instead of vertical. "There you are. You're gorgeous, Mr. MacAllister."

"And you are the most beautiful woman I know," he said, circling her waist with his arms. "I swear, Jillian, you don't look a day older than the first time I saw you in Deede's store autographing your newest book."

"You're such a sweet liar," Jillian said, smiling at him. "Do you like my new dress I bought for this special occasion?"

Forrest followed her and swept his gaze over her from head to toe, nodding in approval at the sea-green, full-length dress his wife wore. It had a scoop neck, cap sleeves and flared slightly from her slender hips.

"It's very, very pretty." Forrest paused. "I'm a nervous wreck about tonight. There has been so much publicity and hype about this event. What if people don't buy Alice's paintings? It will break her heart and... I'm taking a credit card with me.

I'll buy a bunch of her paintings myself if I have to and..."

The telephone on one of the nightstands rang.

"Oh, dear, who can that be?" Jillian said. "We should be leaving right now." She hurried to the telephone and lifted the receiver. "Hello?"

"Jillian? This is Brent Bardow."

"Well, my goodness," Jillian said, "this is a surprise. Are you calling from Wilshire, Brent?"

"No, I'm here in Ventura. I just checked into a hotel, and when they handed me my key card they also gave me a brochure announcing the private showing of Alice's work that's taking place tonight. I didn't know the exact date of it, but the brochure says that it's black tie, invitation only."

"Yes, that's true," Jillian said. "Then the gallery will be opened to the general public tomorrow."

Forrest began to pace around the room. "Brent Bardow. I don't know what happened between him and Alice, but I have a feeling I'm really ticked off at that guy."

"Forrest, hush," Jillian said. "Brent, I certainly don't intend to sound rude, but what are you doing in Ventura?"

"I've come to see Alice," he said. "I've been a total jerk, Jillian, and I'm hoping, praying, that Alice will forgive me. I have to see her. I have to get into that gallery tonight. But…I don't have an invitation and I sure didn't pack a tux. Will you help me, Jillian. Please?''

"What does he want?" Forrest said.

"Shh," Jillian said, flapping one hand at him. "All right, Brent, I'm going to trust you. This is Alice's big night, and I don't want anything to upset her. I'll tell whoever is at the door of the gallery that you're to be allowed in with no invitation."

"Thank you. Thank you so much." Brent paused. "I bet it's too late to rent a tux someplace."

"I'm sure it is," Jillian said. "Don't worry about that. You're crashing the party, per se, so it stands to reason you won't be dressed appropriately. Oh, I hope I'm doing the right thing."

"Jillian," Brent said quietly, "I love your daughter with my whole heart. I want to marry her, spend the rest of my life with her. She's my soul mate, my other half, my partner. I love her. I need her."

Jillian smiled. "I'm definitely doing the right thing," she said, and after finalizing the details with Brent, replaced the receiver.

"Brent and Alice's love is most definitely the right thing, the wondrous thing, that has been the foundation of *our* marriage for over thirty years," she said, slipping her arm through Forrest's. "Brent will be coming to the gallery tonight. The rest is up to them, Forrest. Now, let's go and watch those pretty gold sold-stickers being placed on Alice MacAllister's paintings.''

Brent spoke quietly to the frowning man stationed by the front doors of the gallery.

"Oh, yes," the man said, "Mrs. Jillian MacAllister made arrangements for your admittance but..." He slid his gaze over Brent's black, long-sleeved silk shirt, sans tie, with black slacks. "I guess exceptions are to be made for members of the family of the artist."

"Hold that thought," Brent said. "Pray about that 'member of the family' thought."

"Excuse me, sir?"

"Never mind. Thanks for bending the rules. It sure is crowded in here. Do you have any idea where Alice...Ms. MacAllister is?"

"I believe she's being interviewed by a television anchorman at the moment, sir. Over there, where those bright lights are totally destroying the soft, gentle ambience we created for the paintings being displayed tonight." He sighed dramatically. "Well, the majority of the work has already been sold, but—"

"It has?" Brent said.

"Oh, my, yes. Ms. MacAllister's showing is a huge success, sir. A star has been born."

Brent nodded and attempted to ignore the cold fist that tightened in his gut. He made his way forward slowly, finally stopping at the edge of the group of people watching the interview take place.

Oh, man, he thought, there she was. Alice. She was so beautiful in that rose gown, her dark eyes were sparkling, and her cheeks were flushed, probably from excitement and the knowledge that she had been recognized as a talented artist. This was her night and she deserved to bask in every moment of the attention she was getting.

There she was. The woman he loved. The woman who held his future happiness in her hands. The woman who had given him the portrait in the pewter frame to tell him how much she loved him. He could only hope and pray that he hadn't destroyed her feelings for him.

"Fascinating," the man who was interviewing Alice said, bringing Brent from his thoughts. "Just a couple more questions, please, Ms. MacAllister. It goes without saying that you'll be touring with your work in the United States while you continue to establish your reputation. What I'm wondering is, do you have plans to extend those trips into Europe?"

"No," Alice said, smiling. "I'm not going to Europe. In fact, tonight will be my last public appearance for a very long time."

"I don't quite understand."

"I have no desire to be in the spotlight. Nor do I believe it's necessary. My paintings will speak for me. They *are* me. I simply want to continue to paint, that's all." She laughed. "I'll probably get labeled an eccentric, reclusive artist, but so be it. There are no publicity tours in my future. None."

"One last question—is there a special someone in your life? I'm sure our viewers would like to know."

Alice's smile faded. "I...I'd rather not discuss my personal life. What I mean is—"

"What she means is..." Brent said, making his way forward, "there are just some things that should remain private, no matter how much a successful person is in the public eye." He stopped in front of Alice, who was staring at him with wide eyes.

"I believe that answers the question quite eloquently," the man said, chuckling. He turned to face the camera. "This is Sterling Masters, Channel Fourteen news signing off and returning you to our studio."

The bright lights were turned off, Sterling Masters and his crew hurried out of the gallery, the people who had been watching the interview wandered away, and Alice stood statue-still staring at Brent, her heart racing.

"Brent?" she finally managed to whisper.

"Yeah, it's me," he said, attempting and failing to produce a smile. "I crashed your party with your mother's help. Congratulations on the success of this show, Alice. I sincerely mean that."

"Thank you, but—"

"Is there somewhere we can talk...alone?" Brent said. "Please?"

"Well, I... Yes, we could go into the office in the back of the gallery, but—"

"Lead the way," Brent said, sweeping one arm through the air.

Alice looked at Brent for another long moment, then started across the room with him right behind her.

"Well, Forrest," Jillian said, watching them go, "a very important conversation is about to take place."

"Bardow better not make my baby girl cry," Forrest said, frowning.

Jillian kissed him on the cheek. "Remember, Daddy, there are such things as tears of joy."

* * *

In the small office in the rear of the gallery, Alice snapped on the desk lamp as Brent closed the door behind them. She turned to face him, lifting her chin and meeting his gaze directly as she ignored her trembling legs and thundering heart.

"I'm...I'm very surprised to see you here to-night," she said, wishing her voice was steadier.

"It took me this long to come to my senses, fig-ure things out," Brent said, staying by the door. "It's just a coincidence that I arrived in Ventura on the night of the showing, which is why I'm not dressed properly for it." He paused. "Alice, there's so much I want, need, to say to you. I hope you'll listen, really hear, what I... Will you? Listen to me?"

"Yes," she said.

"When I saw your self-portrait in the pewter frame," he said, "I knew, with no lingering doubt, that you loved me every bit as much as I loved you. I knew that I was wrong, had accused you of things that weren't remotely close to being true."

"But, Brent, it's been weeks since I left that por-trait for you."

"I know. I was still a mental mess, Alice. Yes, I knew then that you loved me, but it didn't solve the problem of your career taking you away from the Island of Wilshire, from me, for weeks at a stretch as you promoted your work.''

"Oh, but I don't intend—''

"Please,'' he continued, raising one hand. "Let me finish.''

Alice nodded.

"I finally put the puzzle together,'' he said. "I remembered how focused I was during all those months I was producing the Renault-Bardow wine. I was centered on my dream and spent little time with my parents, King Chester, my friends on the island. I understand about dreams, Alice, I truly do, but I was so selfish and self-centered I didn't want you to pursue yours at the cost of our being continually together. I was so damn wrong.''

"But—''

"I sat on a hill above the vineyards, the place where I hoped we'd build our home, and I realized that I needed to compromise, be willing to share you with your career, cherish the time we *would* have together. I finally knew, sitting there under the stars, that I would always be there, waiting for you to come home to me.''

"But—''

"Alice, I heard what you said to the man from the television station,'' Brent said, rushing on. "You said you don't intend to tour with your work, that you just want to paint. But I've come here to beg your forgiveness for the horrible things I accused you of. I came here to tell you that you should never give up your dream. I came here to tell you that we could make it work by being partners, soul mates forever. I came here to ask you, again, to marry me, stay with me, until death parts us.''

"Oh, Brent," Alice said, tears filling her eyes.

"You believe me, don't you? You know I'm not just making this all up because I heard what you said to that guy? I swear it's true, Alice. I would be there, waiting for you, every time you came home. I even accepted the fact that we wouldn't have children because you'd be traveling so much. Oh, God, tell me you believe me.''

"I do," she said, a sob catching in her throat. "Yes, I believe you.''

Brent stared up at the ceiling for a moment, to gather his emotions, then looked at Alice again.

"Thank you," he said, his voice raspy. "Will you forgive me for the pain I caused you? Will you paint a portrait of us together, which we'll put in another pewter frame and hang in a place of honor in our home? Will you create babies, little miracles, with me? Ah, my Alice in Wonderland, will you marry me?''

Alice smiled as two tears spilled onto her cheeks. "Yes. Yes. Wait. Let me remember how many questions you asked. Yes. And, oh, yes, Brent Bardow, I'll marry you, be your wife and the mother of our children. Oh, God, Brent, I love you so much."

Brent let out a pent-up breath, then opened his arms to Alice. "Come here, please."

Alice ran across the room and into Brent's embrace, encircling his neck with her arms. They held fast to each other, allowing the depth and the warmth of their love to chase away the chill of loneliness and heartache that had consumed them.

"I love you," Brent said finally.

Alice tipped her head back to meet his gaze, seeing the tears that shimmered in his blue eyes.

"And I love you," she said, her own eyes brimming with tears.

Brent's mouth melted over hers and the kiss sealed their commitment to forever. Desire suffused them and hearts beat in wild tempos of want and need and love.

Brent broke the kiss and spoke close to Alice's lips.

"You'd better get back out there," he said, his voice husky with passion. "This is your night to shine and you deserve to enjoy every second of it.

I'll wait for you until the show is over. I'll wait for you, Alice.''

"I've been here long enough," she said. "I'll leave my paintings behind to speak for me. It's time for me to be with my future husband. It's time to begin our life together so that in the years to come we can stand side by side on the Island of Wilshire and say to each other, oh, look at us. My darling Brent, your Alice in Wonderland wants to go home.''

* * * * *

*Be sure to watch for
Emily MacAllister's story,*

PLAIN JANE MACALLISTER,

*coming only to Silhouette Desire
in September 2002.*

*And now for a sneak preview,
please turn the page.*

Prologue

Home, Mark Maxwell thought as he set his heavy suitcase down. He was finally back in Boston after living and working in Paris for what had proved to be a very long year.

Oh, yeah, he thought, it was good to be home. The research project he'd been invited to take part in had been fascinating and challenging, and it had certainly been an honor, a real feather in his cap, to have been asked to participate.

The problem was his stay in Paris, he mused, had been that the preconceived vision that the majority of Americans had about the city had proved to be absolutely true. Everywhere he'd gone, it seemed, he had been surrounded by couples who were deeply in love.

Maybe the same could be said of Boston, but he'd sure never noticed if it was. He'd gone to Paris with a mind-set, which no doubt made him more aware of the love-in-bloom, or some such thing.

To his own self-disgust, he'd also been thrown back in time to years ago when he, too, had been in love, had lost his heart and youthful innocence to a sweet smile and sparkling brown eyes.

They had made plans for a future together, a for-ever, had talked for hours about the home they would share, the children they would create, the happiness that would be theirs until death parted them.

But none of it had been real...not to her.

She'd smashed his heart to smithereens, leaving him stunned, bitter and determined to never love again.

He'd been convinced that he'd dealt with those painful ghosts, had long since forgotten her and what she had done to him.

But while in Paris in the crush of the clinging couples, the pairs, the twosomes, the old memories had risen to the fore, taunting him, making him face the realization that he really hadn't forgiven, nor forgotten, her.

He strode across the living room toward the kitchen. While he'd been gone, he'd rented his apartment to his buddy Eric, a recently divorced doctor at the hospital, and he'd told Mark on the phone the other night that he'd have some food in the refrigerator for Mark when he returned.

Eric had also said that he'd done as instructed as far as dropping off any mail that looked like a bill at Mark's accountant's office, and that the magazines and junk mail were in a box in the corner of the kitchen.

As Mark scrambled four eggs in a frying pan, adding shredded cheese and hunks of ham, he inhaled the delicious aroma, then frowned as he scooped the mounds of eggs onto a plate and carried it to the table at the end of the kitchen. He poured himself a glass of milk, then settled onto a chair and took a bite of the hot, much-needed food.

But he was still frowning as he stared into space as he chewed, then swallowed.

The same ole Dr. Mark Maxwell, his mind echoed.

Dr. Mark Maxwell, who had avoided becoming involved in any kind of serious relationship with a woman for the past dozen years.

Dr. Mark Maxwell, who had buried himself in his work, was the whiz kid of medical research at only thirty years of age.

Dr. Mark Maxwell, who was still a kid, eighteen years old, wounded and raw, disillusioned, bitter and mad as hell.

"Well, isn't this just great?" Mark said, shaking his head in disgust. "So? Now what, Maxwell? How do you plan to free yourself of her ghost?

"I'll get back to myself on this later," he said, getting to his feet. "Damn straight, I will. But for now I'm not thinking about it anymore because I'm definitely brain-dead."

He went to the box in the corner, snatched up the magazine lying on the top of the pile and looked at the cover.

"*Across the U.S.A.,*" he read, then sat down again and flipped it open.

This was fine, he mused. A mindless magazine featuring human-interest stories of people all over the country.

As Mark took a bite of the eggs, then turned a page in the magazine, he stiffened, every muscle in his body tensing as he stared at the story headline.

"Ventura, California, Cousins Marry Royal Cousins in Romantic, Fairy-tale Fashion," he read aloud.

His heart thundered as he looked at a color picture of a multitude of people whom the caption identified as being the two families…the royal one from the Island of Wilshire and the one from Ventura.

And there she was.

She was standing in the row behind the two recently married couples.

It was *her*.

Mark got to his feet so quickly, the chair fell to the floor with a crash he didn't even hear, his gaze riveted on the photograph.

This was creepy, really weird, he thought frantically. He was fighting an emotional battle over her that he thought he'd already fought and won, and now her picture was staring him in the face?

Get a grip, he told himself, setting the fallen chair back into place and sinking onto it. Maybe this wasn't weird. Maybe this was a…yeah…a sign, a directive, telling him that the only way to be truly free of her was to see her one last time.

Mark picked up the magazine and stared at her picture, seeing the smile he knew so well, the blond hair and big, brown eyes, those lips…oh, those lips that tasted like sweet nectar.

She was so damn beautiful, he thought. She was a mature woman now, not a child of eighteen. She'd gained weight over the years, but it suited her and…really, really beautiful and…

He smacked the magazine back onto the table and pointed a finger at her smiling image.

"Gear up, because I'm headed your way," he said, a rough edge to his voice. "It's payback time, Emily MacAllister."

* * * * *

Beloved author
JOAN ELLIOTT PICKART
introduces the next generation of MacAllisters in

The Baby Bet:
MacALLISTER'S GIFTS

with the following heartwarming romances:

On sale July 2002

THE ROYAL MacALLISTER
Silhouette Special Edition #1477
As the MacAllisters prepare for a royal wedding,
Alice "Trip" MacAllister meets her own Prince Charming.

On sale September 2002

PLAIN JANE MacALLISTER
Silhouette Desire #1462
A secret child stirs up trouble—and long-buried
passions—for Emily MacAllister when she is reunited
with her son's father, Dr. Mark Maxwell.

And look for the next exciting installment of
the MacAllister family saga, coming only to
Silhouette Special Edition in December 2002.

*Don't miss these unforgettable romances...
available at your favorite retail outlet.*

Where love comes alive™

Visit Silhouette at www.eHarlequin.com   SSEBB02

If you enjoyed what you just read,
then we've got an offer you can't resist!

Take 2 bestselling
love stories FREE!
Plus get a FREE surprise gift!

**Where royalty and romance
go hand in hand...**

The series continues in Silhouette Romance
with these unforgettable novels:

HER ROYAL HUSBAND
by Cara Colter
on sale July 2002 (SR #1600)

THE PRINCESS HAS AMNESIA!
by Patricia Thayer
on sale August 2002 (SR #1606)

SEARCHING FOR HER PRINCE
by Karen Rose Smith
on sale September 2002 (SR #1612)

And look for more Crown and Glory stories in
SILHOUETTE DESIRE starting in October 2002!

Available at your favorite retail outlet.

Where love comes alive™

 Silhouette®

COMING NEXT MONTH

#1483 HER MONTANA MAN—Laurie Paige
Montana Mavericks
It had been eight long years since small-town mayor Pierce Dalton chose work over love. Then pretty forensic specialist Chelsea Kearns came back into his life—and his heart. Pierce hoped that one last fling with Chelsea would burn out their still-simmering flame once and for all. But they hadn't counted on the strength of their passion…or an unexpected pregnancy!

#1484 THE COYOTE'S CRY—Jackie Merritt
The Coltons
Golden girl Jenna Elliott was all wrong for hardworking Native American sheriff Bram Colton, *right*? She was rich, privileged and, most shocking of all, *white*. But Bram couldn't help but feel desire for Jenna, his grandmother's new nurse—and Jenna couldn't help but feel the same way. Would their cultural differences tear them apart or build a long-lasting love?

#1485 HIS EXECUTIVE SWEETHEART—Christine Rimmer
The Sons of Caitlin Bravo
Celia Tuttle's whole world went haywire when she realized she was in love…with her boss! Tycoon Aaron Bravo had his pick of willing, willowy women, so why would he ever fall for his girl-next-door secretary? But then shy Celia—with a little help from Aaron's meddling mom—figured out a way to *really* get her boss's attention….

#1486 THE HEART BENEATH—Lindsay McKenna
Morgan's Mercenaries: Ultimate Rescue
When a gigantic earthquake ripped apart Southern California, marines Callie Evans and Wes James rushed to the rescue. But the two tough-as-nails lieutenants hadn't expected an undeniable attraction to each other. Then the aftershocks began. And this time it was Callie in need of rescue—and Wes was determined to save the woman he'd fallen for!

#1487 PRINCESS DOTTIE—Lucy Gordon
Barmaid Dottie Heben…a *princess*? One day the zany beauty was slinging drinks, the next day she learned she was the heiress to a throne. All Dottie had to do was get a crash course in royal relations. But the one man assigned to give her "princess lessons" was the same man she'd just deposed…former prince Randolph!

#1488 THE BOSS'S BABY BARGAIN—Karen Sandler
Brooding millionaire Lucas Taylor longed for a child—but didn't have a wife. So when his kindhearted assistant, Allie Dickenson, came to him for a loan, the take-charge businessman made her a deal: marriage in exchange for money. Could their makeshift wedding lead to a once-in-a-lifetime love that healed past wounds?

SSECNM0702